DRASTIC ACTION!

"This must be where the serious research gets done," Joe said as he and Frank made their way through the medical labs building. As they approached lab five, Joe detected a strange odor in the air. "Do you smell that?" he asked Frank.

Frank sniffed, then made a face. "It's some kind of gas," he said.

As the Hardys walked farther down the hall, the odor became stronger. When they reached lab five, Joe realized that the smell was coming from inside. "Come on!" he cried, pushing open the door.

As he entered, a young man fighting off flames with a fire extinguisher bumped into him. "Get out!" the man cried. "It may blow!"

Only a second later there was a giant whooshing sound. "Get down!" Frank urged, shoving Joe and the young man to the ground.

Joe looked up ___ to see the lab blow apart in ___ on!

Nancy Drew & Hardy Boys SuperMysteries

Available from ARCHWAY Paperbacks

A Nancy Drew AND Hardy Boys SUPER MYSTERY™

TARGET FOR TERROR

Carolyn Keene

AN ARCHWAY PAPERBACK
Published by POCKET BOOKS
New York   London   Toronto   Sydney   Tokyo   Singapore

This book is a work of fiction. Names, characters, places and incidents are products of the author's imagination or are used fictitiously. Any resemblance to actual events or locales or persons, living or dead, is entirely coincidental.

AN ARCHWAY PAPERBACK *Original*

An Archway Paperback published by
POCKET BOOKS, a division of Simon & Schuster Inc.
1230 Avenue of the Americas, New York, NY 10020

ISBN: 0-671-88462-X

First Archway Paperback printing August 1995

10 9 8 7 6 5 4 3 2 1

NANCY DREW, THE HARDY BOYS, AN ARCHWAY
PAPERBACK and colophon are registered trademarks of
Simon & Schuster Inc.

A NANCY DREW AND HARDY BOYS SUPERMYSTERY
is a trademark of Simon & Schuster Inc.

Cover art by Brian Kotzky

Printed in the U.S.A.

IL 6+

TARGET FOR TERROR

Chapter

One

EVEN FROM UP HERE the city takes my breath away!" George Fayne exclaimed to Nancy Drew as their plane began its descent into San Francisco International Airport. "Do you think we'll have any time to explore?"

Nancy took in the view of San Francisco Bay, the Golden Gate Bridge, and Alcatraz. The sky was clear and cloudless; the bay shimmered in the sunlight. As the plane flew lower, Nancy could pick out specific details of the city—big Victorian houses painted in wonderful pastel colors and cable cars clinging to steep hills. A familiar feeling of excitement came over her.

"I love San Francisco," she said, "but unfortunately I doubt that we'll have many chances to sightsee. Soong's uncle, Tim An, made it pretty

1

clear to my dad that we have to stick close to her—at least until he can make it here from Philonesia."

George became serious. "I can't even imagine what it's like to get kidnapping threats."

"It must be pretty awful," Nancy agreed.

Nancy and George had traveled from their hometown of River Heights, Illinois, to California to help out Tim An, an internationally known lawyer and an old friend of Nancy's father, Carson Drew. Mr. An had recently been elected president of Philonesia, a small island nation in the Indian Ocean. His niece, Soong An, was a college student at San Francisco University— and a promising concert violinist. According to Nancy's father, Soong's uncle had received several threats to step down from office. If he didn't, Soong would be kidnapped. Tim An wanted Soong to return to Philonesia, but the young woman had other ideas.

Nancy knew that Soong had a Young Performers Award competition scheduled for the coming Sunday. Her uncle was flying to San Francisco for the competition and planned to convince Soong to return home with him. For Tim An, the trip was risky. Philonesia's political stability was at stake, but Nancy knew the man would do anything to get his niece home. Meanwhile, she and George had to do their best to protect Soong.

"Well, if anyone can get to the bottom of this, you can," George said.

"Thanks for the vote of confidence," Nancy said, smiling. "But Mr. An doesn't want me to find out who's behind the kidnapping threats. He just wants someone he can trust, who's Soong's age, to look after her. Apparently she hated having two male bodyguards following her everywhere. She demanded that her uncle send the guards back to Philonesia. They left this morning, so we're arriving just in time." She hesitated a moment, then grinned. "Of course if we *could* find out who's behind this . . ."

George grinned in return. "I *knew* you couldn't resist the mystery part of this case."

Even though she was only eighteen, Nancy already had a spectacular career as a detective. She'd solved many mysteries with her natural talent for sleuthing.

The plane touched down, and a short time later Nancy and George were exiting the aircraft along with the other passengers. The day before Nancy had spoken to Soong briefly, and the young woman had agreed to meet Nancy and George at their gate at the airport.

"Let's hope we recognize Soong," George said.

Tim An had sent Carson Drew a photograph of his niece, but the gate area was so crowded with disembarking passengers and others waiting that Nancy didn't know if she'd spot the girl.

Beside her, George stood, scanning the crowd. "Is that her?" she asked, pointing to a tall, striking student with long, jet black hair and dark, almond-shaped eyes. Next to her stood a trim, elegant woman with olive skin and dark, curly hair.

"Soong!" Nancy cried, waving.

Soong An was smiling as Nancy and George approached. "It's a pleasure to meet you," she said, extending her hand. "This is April Jost, she's with our consulate. April, meet Nancy Drew and her friend, George Fayne."

April shook their hands in a businesslike manner. In person, Soong An was even more striking than in her photograph, Nancy thought. The young woman had high cheekbones, dark, expressive eyes, and a wide mouth. Soong was tall, and her long, flowered silk skirt accentuated her graceful movements. Nancy almost felt self-conscious about her blue jeans and T-shirt, and the fact that she was a little grungy from traveling. Soong was the kind of girl who probably woke up looking terrific.

Soong said, "After we pick up your bags, April will drive us back into the city."

While they were walking toward the baggage claim area, Soong asked them about River Heights. "You mentioned it is near Chicago?"

"About an hour away," Nancy told her.

Soong smiled. "I was in Chicago just a few weeks ago," she said. "For my debut with the Chicago Symphony Orchestra."

"Wow!" George said. "I'm impressed. Nancy

said you played the violin, but I had no idea you were a prodigy."

"Actually," Soong corrected, "at nineteen, I'm too old to be considered a prodigy."

"In Philonesia, Soong is a very well-known musician," April told the girls in her careful, unaccented English. She adjusted the brightly colored scarf she wore around her neck. "Every time she wins a competition, the news appears in all the local papers."

"Tell me about the Young Performers Award this weekend," Nancy said as they entered the baggage claim area. "How many musicians are competing?"

Soong thought for a moment, then shrugged. "I really don't know, to tell you the truth."

"You're kidding!" George said, stopping short. "I mean, when I'm competing in a sports event, I always know how many people I'm up against."

Nancy smiled. George was a terrific athlete—she'd competed in marathons, swimming meets, even a bicycling championship. Nancy could tell from the bemused expression on Soong's face that the violinist obviously didn't think the comparison held.

"I guess that's the difference between being a musician and an athlete," Soong said. "Or at least one of them."

Around them, people were bustling in all directions through the terminal. Flight announcements blared out over the PA. In the baggage claim area, the passengers from the Chicago flight mingled with those from several other flights. At least three baggage carousels were turning at once.

Nancy led the way to the carousel where their luggage would appear. When they reached it, April checked her watch and announced, "Excuse me a moment, girls. If you don't mind, I have a phone call to make."

After April was gone, Soong sighed and stared off into the distance. Now that she was alone with Nancy and George, Soong became less friendly and more distressed. "I hope my uncle realizes that he's making me feel like a prisoner by having all these people guard me."

Nancy and George exchanged a look. "From what I can tell," Nancy said gently, "he has only your interests at heart."

"Then he should let me be!" Soong announced sharply. Several travelers turned to her so Soong lowered her voice. "You have no idea what it's like having your every movement observed. When the Philonesian guards were trailing me everywhere I went—to classes, to practice, to the dining hall—everyone stared. When I objected, my uncle finally agreed to send them home, but only if you came out to look after me." Soong reached out to touch Nancy's shoulder. "Don't think I'm not grateful, but . . ."

"Of course I don't," Nancy assured her. Privately, however, that was exactly what Nancy was thinking. Soong stepped off to the side while Nancy and George moved in closer to the baggage carousel, ready to grab their luggage when it appeared.

"Why do I get the feeling," George whispered under her breath, "that this is going to be one tough assignment?"

Over her shoulder, Nancy kept an eye on Soong. The Philonesian was standing several feet away, tapping her foot impatiently. Nancy leaned toward George and said, "Because it is."

With a start, the baggage carousel began to move, and behind Nancy, the crowd pressed forward. After several turns of the carousel, Nancy spotted George's blue duffel and her own gray suitcase. She was reaching out to grab her bag when she heard a woman behind her scream.

"Get your hands off me. Stop."

Nancy turned but couldn't see anything through the crowd. Then all at once she caught sight of a young woman being dragged through the airport by a man wearing a rubber mask.

It was Soong An—and she was being kidnapped.

Chapter
Two

NANCY RUSHED through the crowd toward the exit. Soong was thrashing around in the arms of her abductor, trying to get free, but the man's grip remained firm as he dragged her off.

"Hold it right there!" Nancy called out.

The man was across the airport road now, heading for a parking structure. Briefly, he turned around. Soong, who was still struggling, seized the moment. "Let me go," she shouted, and slammed her foot down on her captor's— hard. The man loosened his grip long enough for Soong to break free.

By now, Nancy was across the road. Soong ran toward her as the kidnapper disappeared into the parking structure.

"Are you okay?" Nancy asked breathlessly.

Soong nodded, obviously shaken. She pushed her long, dark hair behind her shoulders and said angrily, "I can't believe the nerve of that man!"

Nancy was amazed at Soong's attitude. She wasn't frightened; she was annoyed. "I don't think he was worried about being polite," Nancy said wryly. Because she'd stopped to talk to Soong, Nancy realized that the kidnapper had too good a head start for her to try to catch him. "Let's go back inside," she told Soong.

Inside the airport, George came running up to them. "Nancy!" she cried. "Where'd you go? I turned around and you were gone."

"Someone tried to kidnap Soong," said Nancy.

"You're kidding," George said, her brown eyes wide with alarm. "How did you stop him?"

"I stomped on his foot," Soong announced proudly. "That made him think twice."

George started laughing, and Nancy smiled. Soong seemed surprised. "What?" she asked. "Did I say something funny?"

"No," George said, her eyes twinkling. "It's just that I have a feeling the guy didn't know what he was getting into, trying to kidnap you, Soong."

Soong arched an eyebrow. "Apparently not," she said. "Or else he wouldn't have tried."

"N-Nancy," George sputtered, pointing over Nancy's shoulder to a group of passengers arriving in the baggage claim area, "you won't believe who's here!"

Nancy turned and saw her old friends Frank and Joe Hardy. The Hardys were from a town near New York City, Bayport, and were also teen detectives. More than once, Nancy had teamed up with them to solve mysteries.

"Frank!" she cried out. "Joe!"

The Hardys came running toward them. The four friends exchanged hugs all around. "What are you guys doing here?" Joe asked.

"We could ask you the same question," Nancy replied, stepping out of Frank's embrace.

As usual when Frank was around, Nancy's heart beat just a little faster. Even though nothing had actually ever gone on between them, Nancy and Frank both recognized that their respect and admiration for each other had an edge of something more, something that could be romantic in a different time and place.

"It's top secret," Frank said, his index finger to his lips.

"Let's call it a working vacation," Joe replied. He stretched and peered over at the baggage claim carousel. "If our luggage ever shows up, that is. I'm going to check it out. You coming, Frank?"

"I'll be there in a minute," Frank called to his brother's back.

Nancy didn't miss the way Frank was staring at Soong. Well, she *was* beautiful, Nancy thought. Still, couldn't Frank be a little less obvious?

"Soong," Nancy said, "I want you to meet my friend, Frank Hardy. Frank, this is Soong An. Her uncle is a friend of my dad."

Soong smiled as she reached out to shake Frank's hand. Frank blushed. "Pleased to meet you," he said. "Do you live here in San Francisco?"

"Yes, I do," Soong said. "For the moment. I'm a student at San Francisco University."

"We're going to be staying with Soong in her dorm," Nancy said.

"You're kidding!" Frank exclaimed. "Joe and I are visiting the campus ourselves."

"You're planning to spend your vacation at school?" George joked.

"Not exactly." Frank peered down at his shoes. "Joe and I are planning to drop in on the dean of students, Bob Harper. He's an old friend of our dad."

Nancy could tell that Frank didn't want to talk about the reason for his visit in front of Soong.

Just then April came striding back to the group, all business. "What's going on here?" she asked, stopping short, apparently surprised to see a young man with Nancy and Soong.

Nancy was quick to introduce Frank to April. "We're old friends," she said. "Frank and his younger brother, Joe, just flew in. Joe's over there, waiting for their luggage."

"I see," April said, forcing a smile. "Needless

to say, I'm always a bit concerned when I find Soong talking to a strange man. Not that I should be surprised."

Soong let out an exasperated sigh. "You might think we were back in Philonesia," she said. "This is the United States. Customs here are different."

"That's not what I meant, and you know it," April said. "It's your safety that is my primary concern. If anything happened to you, your uncle would have my head."

"In fact, something almost did just happen to Soong." Briefly, Nancy told the woman about the kidnapping attempt.

April drew in a sharp breath. "You see, Soong An? I have reason to worry. What if this man had succeeded?" April turned to Nancy. "Were you able to get a good look at the man?" she asked.

Nancy shook her head. "He was wearing a mask, and took off before I could follow him. We should notify the police, though, don't you think?"

"No, no," April said, shaking her head several times. "Soong's uncle has expressly asked me to keep anything involving Soong private and within the consulate."

Nancy decided not to argue with the woman. She must have her reasons to keep Soong's potential kidnapping private. Not being able to go to the police was going to make her own job a lot harder, Nancy thought.

Joe Hardy strode up to the group just then, a duffel bag slung over each shoulder. "Are we ready?" he asked.

Nancy introduced Joe to April. "Is there room in your car for all of us?" she asked April. "Frank and Joe are also heading over to the university."

"Fortunately, I have the consulate's minivan," said April. "Shall we go?"

During the trip from the airport to the university, Nancy, Joe, and George caught up on what had been going on in their lives since they'd last been together. Frank spent the whole time talking to Soong—asking her questions about her concert career, Philonesia, what it was like to be the niece of a prominent political figure. Nancy tried to keep her mind on the conversation with Joe and George, but she kept one ear glued to Frank and Soong's talk. She was surprised that his interest in Soong was bothering her so much.

Quit it, Drew, she thought. Frank Hardy can like any girl he wants. Even though Nancy had a boyfriend—Ned Nickerson—back in River Heights, she couldn't help wishing right then that Frank would pay more attention to her and less to Soong.

Since she was sitting in the front seat, Nancy gave up on the conversations behind her and spoke with April about the kidnapping threats against Soong. "My father told me that Mr. An thinks his political rivals are trying to force him to resign by threatening to kidnap Soong," Nancy said. "Is that true?"

April sighed as she merged the minivan onto the freeway. "The situation in Philonesia is very complicated," she said. "Soong's uncle was elected in a free and democratic process, but there are rebel forces in the north of the island who feel their candidate should have won. These people have genuine concerns—poverty, land rights, fair representation in government—and Tim An will have to answer to them if he is to stay in power."

"You sound as though you're sympathetic," Nancy said.

April raised an eyebrow. "As I said, it's a very complicated situation. I don't agree with the rebels' tactics, if that's what you mean."

"How many threats have there been?" Nancy asked. "Is this the first time someone actually made an attempt to kidnap Soong?"

April concentrated on her driving for a minute, then answered Nancy. "I believe Tim An received two threats in Philonesia. Soong has received three calls, but she couldn't recognize the voice. The most recent calls she described as sounding 'muffled.' But the first call was from someone using a voice disguiser—is that what they are called?"

Nancy nodded and April went on. "But this is the first time anyone has tried to take Soong.

Now, unfortunately, we know that her life is in danger."

"In that case," Nancy said, "it's good that George and I are here. Has anything else happened that we should know about?"

"Yes," April said. "Someone stole a copy of Soong An's class schedule from her dorm room, which means the kidnapper could know where she is to be at any time. Let's just hope you and your friend can protect Soong until her uncle arrives on Sunday."

April pulled off the freeway, and soon they were driving through hilly, tree-lined city streets. After about a mile or so, April parked in front of a complex of redbrick buildings.

Nancy saw college students strolling along the sidewalks. Through a gap between the buildings, she spotted a green lawn where more students were lounging in the sun. People chatted in groups, and the whole campus seemed to be alive with activity.

The Hardys, George, Soong, and Nancy quickly jumped out of the van and unloaded their luggage. They thanked April Jost before she drove off.

"Maybe we should all meet for dinner," Frank suggested, shouldering his duffel bag.

"Sure," Soong said casually. "A group of us meet in the dining hall every day at six o'clock. See you then."

"Great!" Frank exclaimed.

Soong and George began to walk away, and Nancy called after them, "I'll catch up with you in a minute." Then she turned to the Hardys. "Where are you guys staying?" she asked.

"Actually, Dean Harper's put us up in a dorm," said Joe. "Just like real college guys."

"So you *are* doing more than just visiting," she said. "What gives?"

Frank checked with Joe. "I guess Nancy can know about the case."

"Of course I can," Nancy announced. "Don't I always?"

Joe briefly explained why they were at SFU. Dean Harper had been having trouble with an animal rights organization on campus. Their tactics were becoming dangerous, and people had gotten hurt.

"The last thing the group did was set off a smoke bomb in one of the labs," Frank said. "A number of students were hospitalized."

"Sounds serious," Nancy said. "What do they want? What's their goal?"

"Ask us in a few hours," Joe said. "By then we should have cracked the case."

"Right," said Nancy, laughing. "Which dorm are you staying in?"

Frank checked the small notebook he was carrying in his jeans pocket. "Jarman?"

"We are, too!" Nancy exclaimed. "That's where Soong lives."

"So it's a coed dorm?" Joe asked, raising an eyebrow.

Nancy shook her head in mock seriousness. "This is really turning out to be a tough assignment for you, Joe," she said, well aware of how much he loved girls.

"I think I can handle it," Joe said, his blue eyes twinkling.

"If we're in the same dorm," Frank put in enthusiastically, "that means we'll get to see a lot of you and George."

"Right," Nancy said. "Catch you at dinner, then."

As Nancy left the Hardys to rejoin George and Soong, who had waited for her, she wondered if Frank's enthusiasm really had to do with seeing her—or if it had more to do with his being able to spend time with Soong An. Either way, she told herself, it didn't matter. She was here to protect Soong—not to worry about Frank Hardy.

Fifteen minutes later the Hardys had dumped their bags in their room, and were in a meeting with Bob Harper, dean of students at San Francisco University. The dean appeared to be in his late forties, with curly brown hair that he wore long in back and round, wire-frame glasses.

From behind his desk, Harper briefed the Hardys on the situation that had brought them to the university. A group of animal rights activists, calling themselves Ethics Now, had targeted the university's medical research labs. The group wanted the administration to stop all animal testing—for any kind of research whatsoever—and they were using guerrilla tactics to pursue their ideals.

"So far they've set all the animals free, which caused quite an uproar on campus. That was before we agreed to stop testing. Even now they've spray-painted the building and set off alarms and smoke bombs. They've been more than a nuisance." The dean rested his elbows on his desk. "A dozen students had to stay in the health center overnight after the smoke bomb incident. It's becoming quite dangerous."

He leaned back in his chair and focused his gentle blue eyes on the Hardys. "I've tried to negotiate with the group. I've banned testing on all but laboratory rats and mice. I've let them know that even that testing will end soon, but I need time to phase it out." Bob Harper gazed at the Hardys intently. "We're talking about restructuring every aspect of our medical research here," he said emphatically. "We can't do that overnight."

"Do other universities have these problems with animal rights activists?" Frank asked.

"Yes and no," Bob Harper said. He rubbed his eyes. "Most activists accept that testing has to be performed on lab rats and mice. It's the only way advances are possible in medical research. Ethics

Now had accepted this testing until this semester. But since January, the group has called for a ban on all testing, and their tactics have become more extreme."

"Why do you think that is?" Joe asked. "It doesn't make sense when you've already met so many of their demands."

The dean shrugged. "It could have something to do with their leadership or new members—I don't know. So far, we haven't been able to catch a single member of the group in their guerrilla acts. Not everyone in the group is responsible, but I need to know exactly who is. And I need proof."

"It seems to me we've got two angles to investigate," Frank said. "First, the attacks themselves. I think we should head over to the labs. We can talk to the technicians to see what kind of leads they can give us."

"Good idea," Dean Harper said. "What's your other angle?"

"Motivation," said Frank. "We need to find out why Ethics Now changed their tactics and became more outspoken and critical—not to mention destructive—especially when the administration has been cooperative."

"There's one more thing," Joe said. "We should probably stay undercover. That means we need an excuse for why we're looking into the attacks."

Frank nodded his head in agreement. "What if

we go undercover as members of a student group at another university with a similar problem? Our student government asked us to investigate how your administration is handling the attacks."

"Sounds good," Joe said. "That way, if we need to pass ourselves off as students, we can. And we'll also be able to avoid being connected to Dean Harper directly, if that helps our investigation. No offense," he said to the dean.

"None taken," said Dean Harper. He stood up. "I wish I had time to take you boys over to the labs myself, but I can't leave the office right now. If you'll follow me, I'll point you in the right direction."

In the hallway, he nodded toward a cluttered desk. "That's where my assistant, Mike Clark, sits," he told them. "He may be messy, but he's top-notch. If you ever have a problem and I'm not around, talk to Mike. He'll help you."

"Got it," said Joe.

On the front steps of the administration building, Bob Harper gave the Hardys some quick directions. "The med labs are on the north campus, but it's not far," he told Frank and Joe. "You follow the walkway past Jarman and . . ."

As the dean was talking, Frank spotted someone running toward the administration building. The person wore a motorcycle helmet that hid his face. He was carrying a sign in one hand and a can of spray paint in the other.

The sign read Stop Animal Torture!

"Dean Harper!" Frank cried. "Watch out."

The dean realized what was happening, but too late. The masked figure raced up the steps and quickly spray-painted something on the front of the administration building.

"Ethics Now," the person shouted, then turned, and without a second's hesitation sprayed Dean Harper with a blast of red paint— right in the face.

Chapter

Three

MY EYES!" Dean Harper cried, pulling off his glasses. "I can't see!"

For a moment Joe was distracted by the dean's plight, but a second later, he sprang into action. The spray-painting terrorist was already halfway down the steps of the administration building.

"Come on, Frank," Joe cried. "Let's get him!"

The guy took off to the right, toward the university's north campus. Once Joe got a closer look at the person's build, he began to wonder if it was a guy at all. The person had narrow shoulders and long, lean legs. Then he noticed the person's gloved hands. They were small, almost tiny.

The attacker must be a girl!

Even though the spray painter had a head start, Joe kept her in sight. The campus walkways were crowded. Joe quickly darted past groups of students. In front of what must have been a classroom building, Joe got caught behind a throng of people. He moved quickly to circle around the group, but lost the attacker anyway.

"Where'd she go?" Joe asked Frank, who had come to a stop beside him.

"She?" Frank asked.

"It's a woman, Frank," Joe said, panting. "I'm sure of it."

"Over there!" Frank cried, pointing to a walkway on their left.

The attacker was just disappearing out of sight. Joe put on the speed, but the girl had too much of a lead and there were too many people in the way. A hundred yards down the walkway, he stopped. He didn't see her anywhere.

"Where is she?" Frank demanded, panting.

"We lost her," Joe said in frustration. "She knows the campus a whole lot better than we do." He gave a long, exasperated sigh.

"Then let's get back and make sure Dean Harper's okay," Frank said. "Maybe he recognized the attacker."

"With that motorcycle helmet on, I doubt it."

Back at the administration building, workers were already preparing to clean the word *LIARS!* off the front wall. The Hardys found Dean Harper in his office, on the phone. His glasses were off, and his entire face was red, except for two round patches where his glasses had been. His shirtfront and suit jacket were also covered with red paint. While the dean was talking, an idea was forming in Joe's head. He and Frank could go undercover at the medical labs to find out about the Ethics Now attacks, but why not actually go undercover in the organization? What better way to learn about the attacks *before* they happened? That way, too, they could find out exactly who in the group was behind the attacks. Joe wasn't entirely sure the dean, or Frank for that matter, would go along, but it was worth a shot.

"Yes, of course," the dean was saying. "I'm just as eager for this to end as you are, Helen. Okay. Goodbye." The dean hung up, rubbed his red face, and sighed. "I hope you boys can help me out. That was President Gustafson. She says that if I can't bring this to an end, she'll have to find someone who can."

Bob Harper looked down at his red hands, then up at the Hardys. "I have an idea, though."

"So do I," said Joe. He paused for a moment, then said, "We join Ethics Now."

"What?" Frank demanded, staring at his brother. "I thought we had already decided to go undercover as students *against* the kind of guerrilla tactics used by Ethics Now."

"We can do both," Joe said. "Think about it,"

he added, seeing his brother's doubtful expression. "If we join the group, we'll get to know the members personally. We'll find out ahead of time when and where they plan to strike—"

"And you'll be able to learn firsthand exactly what is motivating them to conduct these attacks," the dean finished for him. "That was my idea precisely, Joe," he said, beaming.

Frank considered the idea. "There's only one problem. What if they find out who we are?"

"Then our cover's blown," Joe said. "But until that happens, we'll be way ahead of the game."

"It could work," Frank said thoughtfully. "Meanwhile, it's almost five, and we still haven't gotten to the med labs yet."

Just then the phone on the dean's desk rang, and he lifted the receiver. "Talk to Ida Grossman, she's in charge over there. First floor, Room One-Eighteen."

With that, the dean went back to work, and the Hardys left for the labs. In front of the administration building, Frank consulted a kiosk that had a map of the university.

"We head up this walkway until the end, then take a right at Hill Street," he said. "It's about a block after that."

When the Hardys got to Hill Street, Joe had to laugh. The narrow street went up at a forty-five-degree angle. "Only a block, huh?" he asked. "Lucky it's not farther."

"Streets like this are what make San Francisco famous," Frank told him.

Even though he was in good shape, Joe's legs were aching by the time they got to the labs. The building was at the top of the hill and commanded a great view of the city, east across the bay. To their right, they could see the skyscrapers downtown. Directly below them, Joe spotted the piers of Fisherman's Wharf. Just to the left, he saw boats bobbing up and down in the marina.

Groups of students were sitting around the plaza in front of the medical laboratories, taking in the last rays of sun. Some students were wearing white lab coats, while others were dressed casually in jeans, T-shirts, and denim jackets. Many of them were studying from or carrying thick textbooks.

"Remind me to think twice about college," said Joe. "Those books look serious!"

Inside the building, the halls were quiet. Frank led the way past several open laboratory doors, where Joe spotted students bent over microscopes or peering into petri dishes. The smells of chemicals and disinfectant were familiar from his own biology and chemistry classes.

"Here we are," Frank said, stopping short. "Room One-Eighteen, Ida Grossman, M.D."

Dr. Grossman's office was off to the side of her lab. Through the glass of the lab door, Joe could see the gray-haired scientist bending over her desk. As the Hardys entered the lab, she looked up. "Can I help you?" she called out, standing and walking into the lab.

"We sure hope so," Joe said, introducing Frank and himself. He explained that they were students from the University of Los Angeles, where the administration had been having similar problems with animal rights activists. "Our student government sent us," Joe said. "The president wanted to learn why a group would be involved in these sorts of attacks. We were hoping you could help us."

"Of course," the research director said. "I'm extremely anxious to get to the bottom of this situation before someone is seriously hurt."

"What can you tell us about the attacks?" Frank asked, taking his notepad from his jeans pocket.

Quickly Dr. Grossman gave the Hardys all the information she had. One by one, she recited for them the dates and times of the attacks, and what had happened in each one. Pushing back her gray bangs, she added, "There is only one person who has been present at every incident, and he's a fellow named Jeff Trask. He's not a student at SFU, but was hired as a general lab assistant. He floats among all the labs, taking care of whatever needs to be done. I think he could answer your questions better than I."

"Is it possible that this guy Jeff Trask could be

responsible for the attacks?" Joe asked. "I mean, if he's been present at each one of them?"

Dr. Grossman folded her arms across her chest and thought for a moment. "I've gone over this in my mind dozens of times. I trust Jeff, but the facts are adding up against him. He was working here when the animals got out, he was around when the tear gas went off in the cancer research lab, and he was just quitting for the day when my own office was spray-painted." Dr. Grossman sighed. "I just don't know when our university is going to take some steps. Dean Harper must realize this isn't going to go away. But it's good to know that ULA is taking an active role in their incidents."

"Yeah, they're really on top of the situation," Joe agreed.

"Dr. Grossman," Frank said, "do you think we could talk to Jeff?"

"Not today, I'm afraid," Dr. Grossman said. "He's got a flex schedule, and this is his day off. Hold on a minute." She went into her office and came back with a piece of paper. "He works tomorrow," she said, checking the schedule. "In lab five. That's upstairs. He starts at noon, so you should be able to find him any time after that."

The Hardys thanked Dr. Grossman for her time, then headed outside, where the sun was just beginning to set, bathing the surrounding buildings in a rich glow. A wind had come up and was rippling the trees that skirted the plaza.

"It looks bad for this Jeff," Frank observed. "But I wonder why he wouldn't bother to cover his tracks better?"

Joe understood his brother's thinking. "Either Jeff's not worried about all the circumstantial evidence that's piling up against him, or someone else wants to make him look suspicious. Even if Jeff isn't guilty of committing the attacks, he was around for each one of them, so he should know the most about them, right?"

"Right," Frank agreed. "We'll have to find him tomorrow." Frank checked his watch. "It's almost six," he announced. "We'd better get moving if we're meeting Nancy and George for dinner."

"You're sure there isn't some other reason you don't want to be late?" Joe asked. "Like some tall, beautiful girl, perhaps?"

"What do you mean?" Frank asked, his face reddening slightly. "If you're talking about Soong, she's a talented and fascinating woman—"

"Who also happens to be completely gorgeous!" Joe finished.

"So what if she is," Frank said. "Is that any reason not to like her?"

Joe held a hand to his chest. "Are you kidding? Who do you think you're talking to here? I say, go for it! Just don't let all this take your mind away from our case, okay?"

"Don't worry," Frank grumbled. "You're already making a bigger deal out of it than it is."

Joe wasn't sure, especially once he and Frank met up with Soong, George, and Nancy. Joe watched his brother follow Soong around the dining hall—in line at the steam tables, at the beverage dispensers, and as she walked toward the dining room and looked for a table—and couldn't help thinking that he'd never seen Frank have it so bad for a girl. Oh, well, he thought, one less able body on board!

Two other girls joined them for dinner, and Soong introduced them. "These are my suitemates, Charlene Hilton and Li Bao. Li's also from Philonesia. We have separate rooms in a suite."

"Hi," both girls said as they set their trays down.

Joe noticed Soong peeking around as if she were searching for someone. Suddenly her face lit up. "Erik, we're over here," she called to a tall, good-looking guy with dark, curly hair. He came over to the table. "Everyone, this is Erik Kolker, friend and fellow musician." She introduced the Hardys, George, and Nancy. Erik sat on the other side of Soong and made it clear—at least to Joe—that he and Soong were close friends.

Joe could see Frank was squirming while Erik and Soong talked about the Young Performers competition, which Erik had also entered. He talked intensely about who had the best chance of winning. Frank tried to involve himself in the conversation, but Erik kept cutting him off.

"This guy's something else," Joe whispered to Nancy and George under his breath. "Who dropped him onto our planet?"

George laughed under her breath. "Soong told us Erik is one of her best friends, so watch what you say."

"You're just upset because he's making it impossible for Frank to talk to Soong," Nancy said to Joe. "What's gotten into your brother anyway?"

Joe rolled his eyes. "Don't ask me. You know how it is. Guy meets girl. Guy falls for girl. Guy turns into fool." Joe took a bite of his spaghetti and spoke to Li and Charlene, who were sitting to his right. "So, what's it like to live with a world-famous concert violinist?"

Charlene smiled and leaned forward. A stray lock of curly blond hair fell across her pretty face. "Great," she said, "except for all the interference."

"What do you mean?" asked Joe.

"Apparently, Soong gets a lot of phone calls," Nancy put in. "Requests for interviews, that kind of thing."

"That's not all," Li said quietly. "You realize Soong An has been getting threats."

Nancy leaned forward in her seat. "What do you know about the threats?" she asked.

Li's expression was serious. "I only know what

Soong tells me—that she's gotten several threatening phone calls. It's terrible. I am very worried for her."

"How long has this been going on?" Nancy asked.

Li thought for a moment. "Since shortly after her uncle was elected president. I told her that nothing is worth this risk. You must go home to your uncle, go home to Philonesia. It's too dangerous here." She stared at Soong, who realized her roommate was looking at her.

"Li, please stop!" Soong said, shuddering. "You frighten me when you talk that way. You realize I'm going to stay here, and nothing or no one will force me to go home!"

Erik put an arm around Soong's shoulder. "Don't let it get to you," he said, pressing the girl to him. "I'm going to make sure nothing happens."

Li stiffened as Erik spoke to Soong. "As if anyone could trust you with her life, Erik!" Li said, abruptly getting up from the table. "What a phony!"

With that, Li picked up her tray and stormed off. There was a long silence at the table, which Charlene finally interrupted by saying, "Wow, must be something in the stars, huh?"

Joe laughed, along with George and Nancy. Frank still was acting uncomfortable at the sight of Erik's arm around Soong's shoulder, but he joined in, too. Soong and Erik looked at each other and shrugged.

"So when are you going to play for us?" George asked, trying to break the tension.

"How about tonight?" Erik offered.

"Oh, I don't know, Erik," said Soong. "It's been a long day, and I want to be fresh tomorrow for my rehearsal." Soong turned to the others. "All the competitors get to practice tomorrow with the full orchestra—it's our first real rehearsal," she explained.

"That's exciting!" Frank said. "You must be nervous."

"I don't get nervous," she said.

Joe practically choked on his soda, but Frank didn't seem to mind the comment. "Can't you play for us just a little tonight?" he asked. "I'd like to hear you."

"After dinner we can go back to the dorms and get our instruments," Erik said. "There's a common room downstairs. We can play for you there. Soong?"

The girl thought for a moment and then agreed. "Okay," she said finally, smiling at Erik. "If you want to play, I'll play."

Charlene finished eating first and excused herself. The rest of the group finished their desserts, then gathered up their trays and went to bus them by the dishwashing station. By now, the dining room was less crowded. Some students were lingering over cups of coffee, and others had their books out trying to study, but the high-ceilinged room was much less noisy than when Joe and Frank had first entered, and the workers—some of whom had to be students—were busy taking down the salad bar, cleaning up the beverage station, and busing trays.

The group headed out of the dining hall and next door to Jarman Hall. While Soong and Erik went upstairs to get their instruments, Frank, Joe, George, and Nancy went into the common room. Joe sat down in a deep, comfortable armchair, while the others sat on a nearby couch.

At one end of the room, two students had their books spread out on a large wooden table. At the other, a girl sat in a window seat, writing on a pad.

Nancy and George were busy making plans for the next day. Joe was about to talk to Frank about their own investigation when Soong An came running in, extremely agitated.

"What's wrong?" Nancy asked. "Did something happen?"

"Come—" Soong said, breathless. "In my room. There's a message on my answering machine. It's awful. Come and listen!"

Joe followed Nancy and Soong out of the room, with Frank and George close behind. Upstairs, a door was ajar at the end of the landing. Soong rushed back inside the room and went to the answering machine. As soon as she pressed Play, a woman's voice filled the room.

"Go home to Philonesia, Soong An!" the voice warned. "Go home now! You will not be safe until your uncle resigns."

Chapter
Four

SOONG AN CRUMPLED into a nearby chair. "Why is this happening to me?" she wailed. "Now of all times. How am I supposed to concentrate on my competition with all of this going on?"

Erik Kolker came into Soong's room at that moment. His dark eyes searched Soong's face, and he asked, "What happened?"

"Soong got a threatening message on her answering machine," Nancy said.

She reached over and replayed the message, to be sure there weren't any clues she might have missed. The voice was clearly a woman's, but the person spoke in low, gruff tones, and the words were somewhat muffled, as if the person had put a handkerchief over the phone.

After listening to the message for a second

time, Nancy hit the Stop button. There was no way of knowing if this woman was connected somehow to the man who'd tried to kidnap Soong. One thing was certain—this voice wasn't electronically disguised.

"Do you recognize the voice at all?" Nancy asked Soong.

The young violinist shook her head. "I have no idea who it is."

"You've gotten other threatening messages," Nancy began. "Does this sound like it could be the same person?"

"I can't tell," Soong snapped in frustration.

Both Charlene and Li had come out of their rooms when they heard the commotion.

"It must be," Li offered. "I told you, Soong, it's getting much too dangerous for you to stay in this country. You've got to leave, before the competition. No award is worth putting your life—"

"Li, please." Soong sank her head into her hands. Her long black hair fell over her face. "I simply can't hear any more of this right now."

"Fine," said Li coldly. "So much for my advice. Charlene, I'll be in my room if anyone calls." Before Li left, Nancy noticed that she gave Erik a long, searching look. Then she disappeared into her room that led off the suite's living room.

"Listen," Soong said to Nancy once Li was gone, "I know my uncle thought he was doing me a favor by asking you to come, but I really don't need your help. Now, if you don't mind, I'd like to be alone."

"We understand," Frank Hardy said gently. "Is there anything we can do for you?"

"I can take care of Soong," Erik said to Frank. "I was looking after her long before any of you got here."

"Actually, Erik," Soong said, turning to her friend, "I'd like you to go, too. I really just want to be by myself right now."

Erik acted a bit hurt. "Okay," he said. "That's cool. But I'm right downstairs if you need me."

"Nancy and I are here to make sure Soong is in safe hands," George told him bluntly. "I think we can handle it."

"Please!" Soong practically shouted. "I do not need protection. I'm telling you, these threats mean nothing. I am a grown woman. I can take care of myself, thank you very much."

With that, Soong stormed into her bedroom and slammed the door.

"Whoops," George said. "I guess I said the wrong thing."

"No, you were right," Nancy said. "Soong is obviously shaken up by all this, but she doesn't seem to believe she needs our help. I want to go over to the consulate myself tomorrow and discuss this situation with Wendy Kim, the woman Tim An said I should use as a contact."

"What about Soong?" George asked. "Should I stick around to look after her while you're gone?"

"Maybe we can do it," Frank offered.

"Soong and I have our American civilization class together tomorrow morning," Erik put in. "I can look after her until you guys get back."

"Thanks," Nancy said. "That will help."

"I know I seem overly protective of Soong," Erik continued, "but I'm very close to her, and I'd hate to see anything happen. She's an incredibly talented musician." Erik looked down at his hands, then at Nancy. "Probably the most talented of all of us." He sighed deeply, then headed toward the door. "See you tomorrow."

"Boy, does he have a torch," Charlene said once Erik was gone.

"He's not the only one," Joe muttered.

"What's that supposed to mean?" Frank asked his brother.

"Only that you're prepared to ditch everything to play bodyguard to some exotic violin player," Joe said.

"Time out, guys," Nancy said. "George and I have the situation under control. I think Erik can look out for Soong while we go over to the consulate. You guys have other reasons for being here, right, Frank?"

"Right," Frank agreed. "Sorry, Joe. I guess I wasn't thinking."

"My point exactly," Joe said.

"Come on." The older Hardy dragged his brother toward the door. "We'd better start planning our strategy for tomorrow."

"Now, that's the Frank Hardy I like to hear," Joe joked as they left. "See you, Nancy, see you, George. 'Bye, Charlene."

Charlene was laughing. "Those guys are a kick. What's the deal with them?"

"They're old friends of ours," Nancy said. "We met up with them at the airport."

"Cool," Charlene said. She dropped to the floor and hugged her knees to her chest. "So how about all that psychodrama, huh?"

"What do you mean?" Nancy asked, sitting down on the floor next to her. George joined the two of them.

"Phew." Charlene blew a strand of curly hair out of her eyes. "Li and Erik, Soong and Erik. Frank and Soong. It's like a soap opera."

"You think Frank likes Soong?" George asked, her brown eyes twinkling.

"Oh, please," Charlene said. "Don't tell me you didn't notice."

"He does seem interested in her," Nancy admitted.

"I'll say," Charlene agreed.

"What did you mean about Li and Erik?" Nancy asked.

Charlene looked back and forth between Nancy and George, then lowered her voice. "Li started school in January last year, and she and Erik went out for most of that semester. Then Soong started here in September, and right after that Erik broke up with Li. She hasn't gotten over it."

"Are Erik and Soong going out?" George asked.

"Not as far as I know. Erik's gorgeous, don't you think?" Charlene asked.

Nancy nodded, and George agreed. With his dark, curly hair, and intense blue eyes, Erik was very good looking.

"Soong had a boyfriend back home, but they broke up a few months before she came here. She doesn't like to talk about it," Charlene went on. "I don't think she's ready to get involved again. But you can bet Erik likes her."

"I got that impression," Nancy said. "But if Erik didn't break up with Li over Soong, why is Li so jealous?"

"I don't think Erik ever liked Li as much as she did him," Charlene said. "But even though Erik and Soong aren't going out, they have an incredible bond because of their music. Now that she's here, Erik will never get back together with Li." Charlene stood up. "Well, I have to study," she said. "You guys make yourselves comfortable. Feel free to watch TV, play music, whatever. If Soong didn't tell you, that sofa pulls out into a bed, and it's a double. I'll get you a couple of pillows."

"Thanks, Charlene," Nancy said.

"Yes, thanks a lot," George added.

"What a day," Nancy said as she and George pulled open the bed. "The person we're supposed to guard gets kidnapped, she gets a threatening call, and then she gets mad at *us.*"

"I know what you mean," George said, smiling ruefully. "I can hardly wait to see what tomorrow will be like!"

The next morning Nancy and George had breakfast with a sullen Soong An. The girl's bad mood had only gotten worse, but Nancy decided not to let it bother her. She and George were there to look after the girl. If Soong didn't like the situation, it was her problem, not Nancy's.

Halfway through breakfast, Erik and Li joined them, and the mood only grew more tense, especially when Nancy gave Erik firm instructions for staying with Soong every minute. Finally, after making arrangements to meet Soong in front of the liberal arts building at eleven—after her history class—Nancy and George got up from the table and bused their trays.

"Ouch," said George. "Talk about tense."

"No kidding," Nancy said, glancing back at the table before they left the dining hall. Erik, Soong, and Li were sitting in silence. "If everything Charlene said is true, I don't understand why Li tortures herself by hanging around them."

"Maybe she hopes that Erik will want to get

back together with her," George said with a shrug.

As they headed toward the door, Nancy buttoned the light denim jacket she wore over her white T-shirt. Outside, she pulled a map of San Francisco from her shoulder bag and opened it.

"It looks like we can take the cable car to the Philonesian consulate," Nancy said.

"Great!" George replied. "I love cable cars."

Nancy and George headed toward University Avenue, where the cable car stopped. There, a group of students was also waiting in the bright sunshine of a perfect spring day. After a few minutes Nancy heard the clang of the cable car approaching.

The car slowed to a halt with a noisy grinding sound. George and Nancy hopped up onto a step and grabbed onto the brass railings to pull themselves aboard. A conductor came through the car to take their money, and after another stop or two Nancy and George were able to find a couple empty seats.

Ten minutes later the cable car climbed a steep hill and came to a stop in front of an elegant, two-story limestone building. "This is where we get off," Nancy told George.

Nancy and George hopped off the cable car and walked up the curving driveway. On the front of the building was a bronze plaque that read Consulate General of Philonesia.

Once they were inside, Nancy introduced herself and asked to speak with Wendy Kim, her contact.

"I'll tell her you're here," the receptionist said. "Please have a seat in our parlor. It's down the hall and through the double doors on your left."

The girls went to wait in the ornate parlor. Here, the chairs and sofas were upholstered in green velvet, and there were portraits in gilded frames on the walls. The whole place had a hushed, serious feeling to it, so Nancy was surprised when Wendy Kim emerged. The woman appeared to be in her midthirties. Even though she was wearing a sedate blue suit, she had on funky platform heels and a choker around her neck with a beautiful piece of jade set into it.

"Hi!" Wendy Kim said, reaching out to shake their hands. "What can I do for you?"

Nancy quickly explained who they were. Then she told Wendy about the kidnapping attempt the day before and about the message left on Soong's answering machine.

"I'm glad you came to tell me," Wendy said, sitting down on a couch across from them. "I know President An is very worried about his niece's safety."

"That's why we're here," said George. "To make sure nothing happens to Soong."

"Can you explain the situation in Philonesia to us?" Nancy asked. "It would help us to understand what's happening with Soong."

Wendy took a deep breath. "In a nutshell, rebel forces loyal to President An's predecessor are waging a guerrilla war in the northern part of the country. Their leader, Rupert Tran, refuses to negotiate with our president and will only be satisfied when he resigns. Most of Tran's supporters have gone over to President An's side, but there are still holdouts." Wendy lowered her voice and leaned close to George and Nancy. "In fact, Rupert Tran's own aunt supports President An. You probably met her, since she's Soong's chaperon here in San Francisco."

"Not April Jost?" Nancy said in surprise.

"Yes," said Wendy. "She has worked here at the consulate for quite a while. Some months before the election, she came out in favor of Mr. An. He thanked her by appointing her Soong's chaperon and guardian in the States."

The phone in the parlor rang, and Wendy got up to answer it. She said a few words, then hung up.

"I'm sorry, but I'm afraid I must go," she said. "There's a meeting I must attend. But if there's anything else—"

"You've been a big help," Nancy said.

As Wendy showed them out, Nancy's mind was reeling with the news about April Jost. It seemed strange that Tim An would appoint the aunt of his closest rival to look after Soong, but he must have had a good reason to trust her. Suddenly Nancy remembered how April had left to make a phone call just before Soong was nearly snatched at the airport. What if April wasn't loyal to Tim An after all?

"What gives?" George asked, once they were waiting for the cable car back to SFU. "You're a million miles away."

"In remotest Philonesia!" Nancy joked. She explained to George her suspicions about April.

George let out a low whistle. "You don't think she set Soong up?"

"I can't say," Nancy said. "But it's a lead to pursue. If we're right, Tim An may have made a huge mistake in trusting April Jost."

"Hold on, Nancy," said George. "We're here to protect Soong, remember? Not to figure out who's trying to kidnap her."

Nancy bit on her lower lip. "I know, George. But what if we just happen to solve the mystery along the way?"

"Then Tim An would be pretty grateful."

"Exactly." Nancy smiled. "And it wouldn't matter if I'd done more than I said I would, right?"

"Right." George let out a long sigh. "I should know better than to tell you to resist a mystery."

The cable car arrived a few minutes later, and fifteen minutes after that, Nancy and George were strolling toward SFU's liberal arts building. Nancy checked her watch and saw that it was still a few minutes before eleven. She and George sat down on the steps of the building to wait, and they watched as classes ended and groups of students streamed out. For a few minutes Nancy and George discussed possible theories about April and whether or not she might still be loyal to Rupert Tran.

By ten after eleven, the walkway in front of the building was empty, and Soong still hadn't shown up.

"Where is she?" Nancy wondered aloud, checking her watch for the umpteenth time.

"Maybe she had to talk to the instructor," George suggested.

"I guess that's possible," Nancy said, searching up and down in front of the building one last time. "I don't like the feel of this though. I'd better look for her. You stay here. I'll ask around and see if I can find her class."

Inside the building, some of the classrooms were occupied with instructors and students, while others were empty. Nancy found one where a young instructor was finishing up with a few students.

"Excuse me," she said. "I'm looking for someone. Could you tell me what room American civilization is in? It was a ten o'clock class."

"That's my class," the woman said, smiling. "Who's the student?"

"Soong An," said Nancy. "Tall girl, with long black hair."

The woman nodded. "Soong had to leave class early. Someone came by and said something

47

about a family emergency. She was very upset. Her friend—Erik Kolker—went with her."

Nancy felt her stomach sink. She thanked the teacher, then left the classroom and raced outside.

George, who was standing in front of the building, immediately saw the concern on her friend's face. "Nancy, what's wrong?"

"Soong's gone!" Nancy said, explaining what the teacher had told her. "Oh, George, it's a trap, I just know it."

Unless Nancy was badly mistaken, it seemed as though Soong's kidnapper had struck again, only this time succeeding—and he had Erik, too.

Chapter
Five

WE'LL FIND HER, Nancy," George insisted. "I just know we will."

Nancy didn't feel so confident. "Soong left class early, and she didn't come back at eleven to find us," she said. "What kind of family emergency could have happened? We were just at the consulate. If it had involved President An, wouldn't Wendy have known?"

"I guess so," George said. "But we can't just stand around here doing nothing. We have to look for Soong."

"You're right," Nancy said. "Why doesn't one of us go back to the room and the other search the dining hall? Then we can meet in the quad and search the grounds—if we haven't found Soong."

"We'll find her, Nancy," George said firmly. "Don't worry."

"I can't help it," said Nancy. "I could kick myself for letting Erik stay with her. Her safety is *my* responsibility, plus, if he's with Soong, that means something's happened to him, too."

Nancy and George rushed across campus to Jarman. While George looked for Soong in her room, Nancy searched the dining hall next door. She went through the steam table line, pushing past people buying their lunch early, and walked up and down the dining room itself. There was no sign of Soong.

Back outside, George was waiting, a grim expression on her face. "No luck?" Nancy asked.

"I'm afraid not," said George. "I checked to see if Charlene and Li were there, in case they might know something. But they weren't in their rooms. What do you think we should do next?"

Nancy's mind was racing. "I think we should search the campus, but we'd better call the Philonesian consulate first." She looked around the quad for a pay phone. Suddenly Nancy spotted a familiar face.

Soong An was sitting on the quad's lawn, laughing gaily. Erik, Li, Charlene, and another young man were sitting with her.

"George!" Nancy said, pointing out the group of friends. "There she is, over there."

George turned and saw Soong. "What kind of trick was that?" she asked angrily.

"I don't know," Nancy said. "But you can believe I'm going to find out."

Nancy walked purposefully over to the group. When Soong saw her, she called out, "Nancy, you found us."

"Not before George and I searched your room and the dining hall," Nancy replied testily. "You were supposed to meet us at eleven. What happened?"

Soong tossed her head and smiled. "It was such a gorgeous day, Erik and I decided to bail on class. I told a friend of mine to drop by and say there was an emergency. Can you believe it? That teaching assistant actually let us go."

Erik, Charlene, and Soong all smiled. Li just shook her head and made a face. Nancy was about to say something, but George beat her to it. "You didn't even think about the fact that we'd be worried?"

Soong shrugged. "I guess it didn't occur to me. Sorry."

"What if something had happened to you?" Nancy asked, irritation creeping into her voice. "How were we supposed to know?"

"Erik would have protected me, right, Erik?" Soong said.

"You bet." Erik must have seen the frustration on Nancy's face. "Listen, Nancy, I'm sorry. You're right. It was a dumb thing to do."

"Soong, you don't seem to realize that you

could be in serious danger. Now is not the time to play games—not with me or anyone else."

Soong didn't answer at first. "Okay," she said finally, "I get it. From now on, I'll remember to report to you every time I breathe."

Nancy closed her eyes and counted to ten. Soong An had to be the most exasperating assignment she'd ever had. "That's not the point—"

"Why don't we let it go, Nan?" George said quietly. "I'm sure Soong understands."

There was an awkward pause, which George filled by saying cheerfully, "I've got an idea. It's a gorgeous day. Why don't we all have a picnic lunch? I've heard SFU has great botanical gardens. We can grab some sandwiches from the dining hall and head over there. Maybe we can even toss around a Frisbee. It'll be fun."

Leave it to George, Nancy thought, to save the day. As soon as she heard the idea, Soong's face lit up. Erik and Li seemed eager to do it, too.

"I love to play Frisbee. I've got rehearsal at two-thirty," Erik said, "but I'm free until then."

"Let's do it then. Charlene?" George asked.

Charlene stood up, along with the young man who was with her. "That sounds like a great idea, George, but Stan and I have a meeting to get to. And I have a two o'clock class."

"Maybe some other time," Stan said, putting his arm around Charlene. "See you."

Charlene and Stan strolled off, and George

asked Soong, "Who was that guy with Charlene? He's cute."

"He's Stan Jones," Li said. "He's also from Philonesia."

"Jones?" Nancy asked.

"That's his American name," Soong said, smiling. "I'm not sure what his Philonesian name is. A lot of people do that—take a more Western name once they get here. Li and I met him at a party for the Philonesian students at SFU. There are a lot of us here. SFU is pretty well known back home. Charlene came to the party with me, and the rest is, as they say, history."

As the group headed over to the dining hall, Nancy found herself watching Soong—as she picked out her lunch, flirted with Erik, and said hello to friends. Underneath her tough, exterior, Soong was like any other college freshman, Nancy realized, and only a year older than she herself was. Maybe Soong was just scared and didn't want to think about what might happen to her. Nancy resolved to give Soong another chance.

George managed to get a Frisbee from someone Erik knew, and soon they were ready to go. Soong got in touch with April, to tell her she wouldn't be meeting her on campus for lunch as they'd planned. As they were heading off in the direction of the gardens, the group ran into Frank and Joe, who were standing in front of Jarman Hall.

"Ready for a break?" Nancy asked, greeting them. "We're taking a picnic lunch over to the botanical gardens."

Joe put his hand to his stomach. "Don't mention food. We just stuffed ourselves on burgers and fries."

"Then you won't want to toss the Frisbee around either," George said, pretending to flick it their way.

"No, thanks," Frank said, ducking. "I couldn't keep up with you anyway, George. Not after that performance of yours against Joe in that marathon."

George raised her fist and showed off her biceps. "I could have won, too," she said. "Except there were extenuating circumstances. I had to save someone's life."

Frank laughed and asked the group, "Why don't we meet up later, for dinner or something? Maybe we could go somewhere off-campus."

It wasn't lost on Nancy that Frank was talking pretty much directly to Soong. "Sure," Soong said. "Where do you want to go?"

"I know it sounds touristy, but why not Fisherman's Wharf?" Frank suggested.

Soong smiled and clapped her hands together. "I love Fisherman's Wharf. It's my favorite spot in San Francisco. We can meet at the main entrance to the pier."

"So it's a date," said Frank. "Six o'clock?"

"Sound's great," Nancy said.

"Let's get going!" George insisted. "This Frisbee is burning up in my hand, and besides, I'm starving."

Joe Hardy watched the group disappear and then turned to his brother. "Ready for Jeff Trask?" Joe asked, checking his watch. "He should be at work by now, and I'll bet he can't wait to answer our questions. By the time we're done with him, he won't know what hit him."

"Don't forget," Frank warned as they walked in the direction of the lab. "We don't have any real clues linking him to the attacks."

At the medical labs building, small groups of students were rushing back and forth between the labs on the first floor. On the second floor, however, things were quieter.

"This must be where the serious research gets done," Joe said, searching for lab five, where Jeff would be working. As they got closer, Joe detected a strange odor in the air. "Do you smell that?" he asked Frank.

Frank sniffed, then made a face. "You bet I do," he said. "It's some kind of gas."

As the Hardys walked farther down the hall, the odor became stronger. When they reached lab five, Joe realized that the smell was coming from inside.

"Come on!" he cried, pushing open the door.

As he entered, a young man fighting off flames with a small fire extinguisher bumped into him.

"Get out!" the man cried, warning Joe off. "It may blow."

The young man continued to try to keep the fire under control, but it was impossible. Joe yanked him out of the lab.

Only a second later there was a giant whooshing sound as oxygen was sucked into the fire. "Get down!" Frank urged, shoving Joe and the young man to the ground.

Joe looked up—just in time to see the lab blow apart in a tremendous explosion.

Chapter

Six

FRANK FELT a shower of plaster fall across his back, and all around him fire alarms were going off as the overhead sprinklers came on.

As Frank stood up, he saw that the lab was in flames. He raced to the end of the hall and came back with a fire extinguisher.

"I'm going in," he said to Joe. "Call the fire department."

Frank lifted the fire extinguisher in front of him. He fought his way through the rubble in the doorway, then shot several blasts of foam from the extinguisher at the nearby flames. The heat from the fire was incredible. Behind him, he could hear people shouting and a lot of other noise. He started coughing from all the smoke, but kept on fighting the fire.

Suddenly Joe was at his side, his face sooty, the young man's fire extinguisher in hand. "You think I'd let you do the macho thing all by yourself?" he asked, smiling. "The firefighters should be here soon."

Together, the Hardys fought the blaze. At first it seemed impossible. The fire had quickly spread from the lab bench, where Joe had first seen the young man trying to put it out, to wooden chairs, papers, books. However, Frank and Joe managed to make some headway.

After what seemed like ages there were suddenly half a dozen firefighters in the room with a hose and more extinguishers. Within another few minutes, the group had the fire under control. Frank and Joe headed out of the destroyed lab, then stopped at a nearby cooler for water.

"You kids were pretty brave," the fire chief said, coming over to them. "What happened?"

Frank quickly explained about the young man at the lab bench. "The fire had already started when we got here."

"You think the kid started it?" the fire chief asked.

Frank and Joe looked at each other. "Well," Frank said, "he *was* trying to put out the fire. . . ."

"He could have started it accidentally," Joe added.

"We'll have to check it out," the chief said. "Do you see him around?"

The hall was crowded, but Joe didn't see the young man.

"Looks like he split," Frank said, coming to the same conclusion. "If you'll excuse us, Chief, I want to call Dean Harper and let him know about this."

Frank and Joe went to the public phone at the end of the hall, and Frank quickly put in his call to Bob Harper.

"I know all about it," the dean said with a sigh when Frank got through to him and told him. "I just got a call from Ethics Now. They take full responsibility for the action. You boys were there. What happened?"

"We may have a suspect," Frank confirmed. "According to Dr. Grossman, there's one worker who's been on the scene at every attack. We think he's the same guy we saw in the lab just as the explosion happened. If we're right, his name's Jeff Trask."

"At least that's a start," Bob Harper said. Frank could hear the weariness in his voice. "Let me know if you get any solid evidence against Trask. I'll want to question him."

"No problem," said Frank. "Joe and I are on his trail."

Frank hung up the phone. Joe was waiting expectantly, a colored flyer in his hand and a smile on his face. "Guess what I found," he announced, handing the sheet to Frank.

"'Are you against the cruel and inhuman

treatment of innocent animals?'" Frank read aloud. "'Do you think the university's medical labs should stop their animal testing? Then join us. We are an activist group committed to the rights of innocent animals. We believe the testing on these animals should end. We welcome new members. Meetings every Friday at one o'clock, basement of the student center. Find out how you can make the difference. Ethics Now.'"

"So, what do you think?" Joe asked. "You want to become an animal rights activist?"

Frank looked up from the flyer and thought for a moment. "I told you before, this is risky," Frank said. "We could blow our cover here at the med labs in a second. You're talking about *two* undercover assignments. That's pretty tricky."

"It's the only way to find out who's involved," Joe said. "I'll bet you anything our friend Jeff Trask is heading over there right now."

Frank handed the flyer back to Joe. "Okay," he agreed. "But let's keep a low profile, all right? No volunteering for their next mission."

"Scout's honor," said Joe, giving his brother a mock salute.

The meeting in the basement of the student center was just getting under way when Frank and Joe walked into the room. Folding chairs were arranged in a circle. About twenty people were sitting or standing, and two men seemed to be running the meeting.

"Come on in!" said one of the men. He was a ruddy-looking, gray-haired man in jeans, a denim shirt, and a flowered tie. "Welcome to Ethics Now," he called out. "I'm Mike."

"I'm Stan," said the other man, a tall, thin guy with short, jet black hair.

"I'm Frank, and this is Joe," Frank said, waving hello.

"Glad you could make it," Stan said to them. "Have a seat. We'll start in a couple of minutes."

Frank and Joe found two seats together. As Frank waited for the meeting to begin, he scanned the members of Ethics Now who were sitting in the circle. Frank looked for the young man they had seen in the lab. He wasn't there, but Frank almost fell out of his chair when he saw who was.

"Look, it's Charlene," Joe whispered to his brother at the same time that Frank spotted Soong's roommate. "What's *she* doing here?"

Charlene had had her back to the circle, talking to someone behind her, when the Hardys entered, which was why neither of them noticed her at first. At the moment she was too busy taking notes to see them. Her head was bent over, and her curly blond hair hid her face from view. Frank knew it was only a matter of time before she recognized them. Although she didn't know that the Hardys were at SFU to investigate Ethics Now, she did know that they were Nancy's friends and that they weren't students at the university.

"What should we do?" Joe whispered to his brother.

"There's nothing we can do," Frank said. "We'll just have to hope she doesn't wonder what *we're* doing here."

"If she starts asking questions, we'd better have a good bluff," Joe said.

Mike called the group to order. "We're ready to start," he said. "Stan and I have the leadership roles this week, so we'll be running this meeting. Can I have your attention?"

Charlene looked up from her pad, saw the Hardys, and blinked several times in confusion. Frank saw her open her mouth more than once, as if she were going to say something, but finally she smiled at them and gave them a friendly shrug. Frank let out a sigh, and Joe whispered, "At least we passed that test."

"Welcome to Ethics Now," Mike said. "For our newcomers, I want to go over some of our bylaws. First, we are committed to the humane treatment of all animals. We believe in vegetarianism. We do not wear leather—"

Frank looked down at his leather high-tops, then realized that the other members of the group were all wearing canvas sneakers or some other kind of shoe besides leather. He began to feel a bit uncomfortable, especially when he thought about that burger he'd had for lunch.

"We are against animal testing in all forms."

"Right!" a young woman shouted.

"Including lab rats and mice," Stan added. "This is a new policy this semester, and it has the full support of all our members."

"You bet," a few people chimed in. Frank noticed that other people remained silent. Obviously, there was disagreement within the group.

"We do not condone violence, but we do condone sabotage. If one act of sabotage can free one animal, then it is worth the cost," Mike finished. "So far, does this sound like your kind of group?" he asked the Hardys.

Joe nodded several times, and Frank joined in. "You bet," he said. Frank was excited. Already a member of the group was talking about sabotage.

"One other thing," Mike said. "We have a confidentiality rule. Nothing that is discussed in the meetings is to be talked about with anyone outside the group. Also, since our group depends on anonymity, we never discuss who our members are."

"No problem," Frank said. Secretly he was relieved. The confidentiality rule would keep Charlene from mentioning to anyone that he and Joe had joined Ethics Now.

"Tell us a little about yourselves. What brings you here?" Mike asked. "How did you find us?"

Before Frank could speak up, Joe was babbling away. "I'm Joe, and this is my brother, Frank. We're from southern California," Joe told him. "My brother and I surf, and we're totally upset by what we see in the ocean. You know, sick seals, and the underground testing that deafens the whales. Not to mention net fishing. We joined a local group, and now we're traveling around to see what other groups do."

"Cool," Mike said, smiling. "I like your style, guys. Welcome."

"Thanks," said Frank. "Good going," he whispered to his brother. "I like your style, too."

"I have a problem," said Stan. He leaned forward in his chair and looked at both Hardys with his cool, dark eyes. "If these guys want to observe, which is fine with me, then I think they have to agree to our initiation."

"Which is?" Frank asked.

"Nothing major," a young man with long hair said.

"Paul's right. It's just a way of proving loyalty," Mike said. "Don't worry."

"What do we have to do?" Joe asked.

"Something that will give you a real idea of activism," Stan said, his voice rising with enthusiasm. "Mike's mentioned that the group condones sabotage. So that we know we can trust everyone—even observers—not to reveal our tactics or our activities, we ask that they join us."

Frank looked at Joe. He didn't like the way this was going.

"To prove your loyalty," Stan said, "you and your brother will commit our next act of sabotage against the university."

Chapter

Seven

JOE HARDY SQUIRMED in his seat. So he and Frank were about to become terrorists. Dean Harper wasn't going to be happy to hear about this.

"Nice going, Joe," Frank whispered to his brother. "This is some serious hot water. Very hot water."

Joe shot his brother a look. "You think I like it?" he asked under his breath. To Stan, he said, "You don't mean doing something illegal?"

Stan frowned. "We like to think of our work as causing nuisances. We try to avoid anything that would directly involve the police—or any kind of investigation."

"Well, what about that explosion today?" Paul,

the long-haired guy, asked. "There was a lot of damage from that. I heard the fire department is going to investigate."

There were murmurs of concern throughout the room.

"That was a mistake," Stan said. "We didn't expect it to get out of control. Now, back to our new members—"

Suddenly Charlene stood up. "I thought we agreed last week to put any new actions to a vote," she said, addressing the group as a whole. "Even initiations. Wasn't that what we agreed?"

Some members of the group spoke among themselves. Others looked uncomfortable.

Stan stared at Charlene. "You're not coleader this week. The current coleaders get to decide how to handle all actions and all initiations."

"Charlene's right, though," Mike said. "We did decide to hold a vote for each new action, right?" He scratched his head. "So I guess we should put this one to a vote."

The group stopped talking for a moment. Then Paul spoke up. "Okay, let's vote. Do we ask Frank and Joe to commit an action or not?"

One by one, Mike polled the group. To Joe's surprise, Charlene voted no. But a majority of the group voted yes.

"That's decided then," said Stan. "For now, we go ahead with the action."

"Since we're following our old policy, the rules

are as follows," Mike added. "All instructions are given anonymously, and all actions are done by an individual acting alone and taking sole responsibility for the action."

"That way, if the person gets caught," Stan went on, "the rest of the group is protected. You won't know who gives you your instructions."

Joe nodded, but he had a pretty good idea who was in charge—at least for now. If this meeting was any indication, either Stan or Mike would be the one to call.

"In your case," Mike said, "we'll let you commit your action together."

"Thanks," Joe said, not meaning it. He met Charlene's eye, and she returned his gaze intensely.

"I bet you guys didn't expect this when you walked in the door," Mike said.

"Actually, no," Frank said. "I guess we had demonstrations in mind, or protests. That sort of thing."

"We take our ethics very seriously," Mike replied. "And since Stan joined us, we've gotten even more active. Some coleaders don't agree, but he's convinced us to take a strong, subversive role. I think the university is starting to listen."

You bet they are, Joe thought. More than you think.

For the rest of the meeting, Mike and Stan led the group. A young woman with her hair in a single thick braid stood up and gave a report on Heal the Bay, a subcommittee of Ethics Now that was looking into pollution in San Francisco Bay.

"That's something you boys might want to get into," Mike told the Hardys when the woman was done.

Joe smiled. "Yeah, sure," he said.

"We could use more help," the young woman said. "Not all of us are interested in the medical labs," she said pointedly. "Some of us feel there are other issues."

"You'll have your turn when you're coleader," Mike said.

The meeting broke up soon after that, and Frank noticed that Charlene went over to Stan to give him a hug as she headed for the door.

Before they left, the Hardys wrote down their phone number for Stan. "We're staying in Jarman," Joe said. "With a friend," he hastily added. He didn't want Stan questioning why two students from out of town would be staying in campus housing. He also gave him their room number. "When can we expect to hear from you?"

Stan shrugged. "That depends on what the group decides. We have to determine the action, and then someone will contact you." He smiled. "Don't worry, guys. It won't be too long."

Outside the student center, the sun was shining, and there was a cool breeze blowing off the bay. Ordinarily, Joe would have felt ecstatic on such a glorious day. Right then, though, he wanted to crawl into a hole.

"I know, I know," he said to Frank as they walked back to their dorm. "Bad idea. So shoot me. How else were we going to make any headway in our investigation?"

"I can think of half a dozen ways," Frank said, sputtering with anger. "How are we going to break this news to Dean Harper?" he demanded. "And what if we get caught? How will we explain it to Stan and Mike when the administration decides to let us go? This is a real problem, Joe."

He started moving faster, and Joe had to race to keep up with him. Around them, students rushed to their afternoon classes. For the first time since he'd gotten to SFU, Joe envied them. Studying night and day would be better than dealing with an angry brother, especially if his name was Frank Hardy.

"I understand that," said Joe. "But what do you want me to do about it? We've got to stay with the plan now. We don't have a choice."

"Believe me, I know that," Frank said. "But I'm not happy about it. What do you propose we tell Dean Harper, for example?"

"The truth," said Joe. "That we're closer to finding out the specific members of Ethics Now who are behind the attacks on the medical labs." He paused for a moment, then tried to make a joke out of the situation. "And that we're going to stage the next attack."

"Very funny," said Frank. "You can be the one to deliver the good news."

At the university's botanical gardens, Nancy, George, Soong, Li, and Erik were just finishing lunch. George, Li, and Erik tossed the Frisbee back and forth, while Nancy chatted with Soong about her life back in Philonesia. Nancy felt herself honestly liking the young woman for the first time. When Soong spoke about her country and life there, she was happy and enthusiastic—that was, until she reached the point in her story when she left Philonesia. Then a sadness crept into her voice.

"I left much behind," Soong said wistfully.

"You mean your family?" Nancy asked.

"There isn't much of my family left, but some. There are a few others—friends." Soong tossed back her jet black hair and forced a smile. "But I try not to think about this. I'm here to further my career. For now, that is all that matters."

Erik, George, and Li came back to the picnic area. Erik flopped down beside Soong, breathless. "What a blast!" he announced. "For ten whole minutes I didn't think about the competition or all the pressure." His expression became serious and more intense. "Now, of course, I'm back to hearing the music in my ears and worrying about my chances."

71

"You have a very good chance, and you know it," Soong said.

"Only if I can beat the odds-on favorite," Erik replied.

"Who's that?" George asked, sipping sparkling water from a bottle.

"Soong An!" Erik announced. "My best friend and chief rival. No matter how much I like you, Soong, I still want to beat you."

For a moment Nancy saw the doubt that Erik was feeling pass over his face. Beneath all his blustering, Erik was really worried about the competition—more worried than Soong.

"That is, if nothing happens to her between now and then," Li said.

"Why must you always be the voice of doom, Li Bao?" Soong demanded. "I think you'd be the first person to dance at the airport if I left."

"I only want what is right for you, and for our country," Li said sincerely. "Your uncle needs you by his side, and he worries about your safety. That is all that matters to me, Soong."

There was an awkward, tense silence. Finally, Erik stood up and put on his sunglasses. "Well, I'd better go," he said. "My rehearsal's in an hour. I don't want to be late, or else Miles will drop me."

"I'll go with you," Li Bao piped up. She smiled cheerfully and began packing up.

"You don't have to," Erik said. "I mean—"

"Don't worry," said Li. "I want to. I don't

have class till four, and I want to be there to cheer you on."

"Miles will be there," Erik said. "Really, it's unnecessary."

Li wouldn't take no for an answer. It was pretty clear to Nancy that Li really wasn't over her crush on Erik and that she'd do anything to hang out with him.

"Who is Miles?" Nancy asked.

"Erik's manager," Soong said, raising an eyebrow. "Erik's not even a professional, and already he's got people managing him. Maybe I'm the one who needs to worry."

Erik laughed. "Maybe. With Miles on my side, there's no stopping me. Well, see ya."

"So long," Nancy said, watching Erik leave with Li. "When is your rehearsal?" she asked Soong.

"Not until three-thirty," Soong said. "But I do want to hear Erik's rehearsal. I guess I should head back to the dorm soon."

George, Nancy, and Soong threw away the remains of their lunch. Then the three of them strolled through the botanical gardens, taking the long way back through the extensive rose gardens.

"I miss all the flowers of my country," said Soong sadly. "Just after it rains, the air smells of jasmine and pikake." She drew in a deep breath. "I'll always remember those sweet scents, no matter how far away I am."

"Maybe you'll go back," George suggested.

"Maybe," said Soong. "But I doubt it. My parents are dead, and I have very little family there other than my uncle. You cannot understand the troubles my country is going through and how they can affect you, every day of your life, if you live there. I cannot be a musician and live in Philonesia. That is that. So when my uncle pressures me to return, all I can do is tell him why I must be here."

Nancy better understood the tough act Soong put on. The girl was obviously homesick, but also determined not to go back. It couldn't be easy.

When the girls reached Jarman, they ran into Erik and Li, who were just leaving. Erik had stopped to pick up his violin. After a brief conversation with Erik and Li, the girls went up to Soong's suite.

Soong arrived at the door first, with Nancy and George just behind. Suddenly Soong stopped short and turned to them both. She was wild-eyed and shaking.

"This . . . is . . . out of control," she managed to say.

"What's happened?" Nancy asked.

Soong pointed to the door. Nancy saw a note there, along with a doll.

"I don't understand—" Nancy began.

Taking a closer look, she realized why Soong An was so upset. The doll had long, dark hair and was holding a plastic violin. There was a knife stuck through the doll's chest.

George came up to the door and read the note aloud. "'This could be you, rag doll. Tell your uncle to step down. Or you'll be one very sorry girl.'"

Chapter
Eight

Soong collapsed against the wall. "Why is this happening to me?" she wailed.

Nancy could tell that the seriousness of her situation was finally registering with Soong. George took Soong's keys from her and opened the door.

"We'll find out," Nancy assured her. She yanked the doll and the note from the door. Once inside, Soong sank onto the couch, her head in her hands. "Who is my enemy here? Who is doing this to me?"

Nancy thought immediately of April. "Didn't you call April before our picnic?"

Soong nodded. "But you don't think—"

"April's nephew is Rupert Tran," George stated flatly.

"I realize that," Soong said quietly. "Philonesia is a small country, and Tran is my uncle's enemy. But I cannot believe that April—"

"Would set you up for kidnapping?" Nancy finished for her. She gave Soong a long, grave look. "Believe it. Anything is possible, and we don't necessarily have any reason to trust April. At the airport when you were almost kidnapped, April knew exactly where you were. This time, she knew you were out of the dorm. She could have hired someone to deliver the doll, or she could have done it herself."

Soong shuddered. "She's my chaperon. My uncle has entrusted me to her care. How could she betray that trust?"

"We can't know until we have evidence," Nancy said. "I'll have to watch April while we keep an eye on you. Meanwhile, I think your uncle should know about our suspicions."

"He will be very sad to hear this," Soong said. "As I am," she added. "I don't want to lose April, and I wouldn't want her to be sent home. Isn't there any way we can wait before telling my uncle?"

Nancy was surprised by Soong's reluctance. She ought to be worried about the possibility that April wanted to have her harmed. Instead, Soong was also concerned about Tim An making April return to Philonesia.

"I don't think we should wait," Nancy said.

"We have reason to suspect her, and your uncle should know."

"If you say so." Soong stood up and gave a wan smile. "I'd like to head over to the concert hall to find Erik, if you don't mind. He seems to be the only one who can calm me down these days. Besides, I don't want to miss his rehearsal."

As Nancy and George headed over to the concert hall with Soong, Nancy was thinking about this latest turn. Something wasn't clicking for her. April had said the first threatening call Soong got came from a disguised male voice. But the call the night before was definitely from a woman. The threat on Soong's door didn't have to do with kidnapping. It was more of a warning, and it had to do specifically with Soong convincing her uncle to step down. Maybe April Jost was on her nephew's side, working against Tim An. It was worth considering.

On the way over to the concert hall, Soong was unusually subdued. Hammond Hall was an ornate, marble-fronted building across the street from the main campus. Once the girls entered the cool, high-ceilinged hall, Soong grew silent. Nancy watched as she lost herself in the music inside the hall.

The three of them walked through the marble lobby to the hushed auditorium. Onstage, the orchestra was just beginning a brooding, melodic piece. Erik was standing near the conductor, playing the first soft notes of what was an intense —and very difficult—violin part.

Silently, with her eyes and ears trained on Erik and the orchestra, Soong walked to the front of the hall and sat down on one of the deep-cushioned, velvet seats. Nancy and George followed and took seats flanking her.

For the next fifteen minutes, Nancy lost herself in the music and in Erik's seemingly flawless performance. When it was over, the audience— about fifty people scattered around the hall— clapped appreciatively.

"That was great!" Nancy told Soong. "Erik's good."

"Yes," Soong replied, her expression serious. "He made a few errors, but that was a solid performance. He should be able to correct them tomorrow."

"I want to call the consulate and leave a message for Soong's uncle," Nancy said to George. "You stay with Soong."

"Will do," said George.

"Nancy," Soong said, stopping her before she could leave, "I want to talk to the conductor. After you make your call, would you mind going back to my room and getting my violin?"

"Not at all," said Nancy. "I'd be happy to."

Soong An handed Nancy her keys and told her where she'd find the instrument. "Be very careful," she said. "It's priceless, you know."

"Great," said Nancy, rolling her eyes in mock reluctance. "First I have to protect an incredibly important dignitary's niece. Then I have to carry her priceless violin. What's next?"

"The crown jewels?" Soong suggested with a wry grin.

Nancy found a public phone in the lobby of the building. As she punched in the numbers, she noticed Erik Kolker hurrying out of the concert hall with Li Bao. Nancy wondered for a moment where they were going, then was connected to Wendy Kim at the consulate. When Wendy heard about the latest incident, she expressed her concern.

"This is very serious," Wendy said. I will certainly let President An know. Is there anything else I should tell him?"

Nancy shared her worries about April Jost. "Perhaps it's just a coincidence," Nancy said, "but April's had the opportunity to set up both the kidnapping and this latest event."

Wendy drew in a sharp breath. "I understand. April's not here at the moment, and this doesn't seem to be something I can bring up with her directly, but I will tell the president when I call him. In the meantime, we'll just have to keep a close watch on her and see if she trips up."

"That's exactly what I was hoping you'd do," Nancy said.

"Keep in touch," Wendy said, hanging up.

Nancy had just replaced the receiver, when she

saw April herself. The woman was standing in a corner of the lobby, talking in low tones to a good-looking young man who appeared to be Philonesian. The man seemed to be insisting on something, and as far as Nancy could tell, April was trying to put him off. Finally the young man ran a hand through his dark hair before turning and walking out of the building. Nancy stepped toward April, who gave a start when she saw her.

"Oh, Nancy," April said, "how are you? How is everything?"

"Fine," Nancy responded shortly. "Who was that you were talking to just now?"

April looked behind her at the door the young man had disappeared through. "He's—he's a relative of mine, actually. He lives here in San Francisco."

"That must be nice for you," Nancy said.

To herself, she wondered if he was also related to Rupert Tran? Was he the man who had attempted to kidnap Soong? He was the right height, Nancy thought. Too bad the man had been wearing a rubber mask.

Realizing she had a terrific opportunity to follow the guy, Nancy quickly said goodbye to April and headed outside. Of course, she remembered, she had to pick up Soong's violin, but she could do that afterward. She still had time before Soong's rehearsal.

A bank of clouds had come rolling in from the bay, and the sunny sky was now gray. Nancy raced down the stairs to the sidewalk, but she did not see the young man. She walked several blocks in both directions, but there was no sign of the guy. Finally she gave up and headed over to Soong's dorm. There, she was surprised to find that the door to the suite was ajar.

Nancy pushed the door open. "Is anyone here?" she called out quietly. When no one answered, Nancy stepped into the living room and walked down the hall to Soong's room.

There Nancy gave an involuntary gasp of surprise. Erik Kolker was standing by Soong's bed, with an open violin case before him. In his hands was a violin bow—the strings had been cut from it.

Erik Kolker had ruined Soong's prized instrument.

Chapter

Nine

"N**ANCY**!" E**RIK CRIED**, turning to her. "Look at what happened. Someone destroyed Soong's bow. They cut the strings."

Nancy drew in a sharp breath. Turning her eyes from the mangled bow, she spotted a red penknife lying on the bed next to the open violin case. Next she studied Erik, searching his expression for any sign of guilt. He seemed genuinely surprised and shocked.

"Who would do this?" Erik demanded hotly. "This is Soong's favorite bow. She calls it her good luck charm. I know I'd have a hard time performing well if this happened to me."

Exactly, Nancy thought. She didn't want to jump to conclusions, but she knew one person who had a lot to gain if Soong An was too upset to turn in a good performance. And Erik knew the bow was Soong's good luck charm.

Then Nancy noticed an index card propped up in front of the violin case. It was typewritten. She leaned closer and read it aloud: "'We know where you are, Soong An, and when. We'll keep sending you these messages, until you convince your uncle to resign. Go home, Soong An, or face the music.'"

A shiver went up Nancy's spine. This note had a lot in common with the doll Soong An had just received. But once again, Nancy had the distinct impression that she was dealing with something different from the kidnapping—although the two events could be related. The ultimate goal of both was for Soong's uncle to resign—either because of kidnapping threats or because Soong would become so distraught her uncle would be forced to give up.

Of course, there was another possibility as well, and that involved Erik Kolker.

Nancy stood back, folded her arms across her chest, and said to Erik, "Tell me exactly what happened. You left the concert hall with Li—"

Erik seemed surprised. "How did you know?"

"I was in the lobby making a phone call," Nancy explained. "I saw the two of you."

"I promised Soong I'd get her violin," Erik said.

"But Soong asked *me* to get it," Nancy said, confused.

"I know." Erik shrugged. "But she said you had something else to do first. Also, she decided she needed to spend some time backstage warming up, so she wanted me to get it right away. I stopped by my room to drop off my instrument, and then came here. When I got here, the door was open. And this is what I found."

"What about Li?" Nancy asked evenly. "What happened to her?"

"She went upstairs right away when we got to the dorm," Erik said. "But when I came by she was gone."

In the hall Nancy heard a young woman's voice. "Look—the door's open now. I think there's someone inside," the voice said.

"Stand back, miss," a man's voice replied. "Who's in there? This is campus security."

Nancy left Soong's bedroom and went into the living room. She found herself staring at a beefy campus security officer and a very frightened Li Bao.

"Oh, Nancy!" Li cried, the relief on her face evident. "I thought you were a robber."

"What's going on here?" the campus police officer asked.

Nancy quickly explained how she'd arrived at the suite to find the door ajar and Erik inside Soong's room. "Someone's tampered with a violin bow in there," Nancy said.

The guard looked at Nancy quizzically. "You don't say?"

Erik emerged from Soong's room with the destroyed bow in his hands. When Erik saw the officer, his dark eyes reflected his worry. "What's going on here?"

"One of the girls who lives here, Soong An, is a concert violinist," Nancy told the officer. "She's participating in the Young Performers competition at Hammond Hall. Obviously, whoever broke in wanted to ruin Soong's chances in the competition." Nancy turned to Li. "Erik said you came up here when he left you. What happened?"

A frightened Li held her hand to her mouth for a moment. "I came upstairs and found the door unlocked and open just a little. None of us leaves the door open!" she said intensely. "I called out Charlene's name, but she didn't answer. I got scared that someone had broken in, so I went for the campus police."

"Before you left, did you hear anyone inside?" Nancy asked.

Li shook her head. "I don't know. I just didn't even want to stay to find out. Do you think the person who ruined Soong's bow was here when I found the door unlocked?"

"It's possible," Nancy said, avoiding Erik's gaze. She still didn't trust that Soong's own best friend hadn't tampered with the bow. If anyone had a reason for wanting to see Soong out of the competition, Erik did.

Nancy bent to examine the lock, while Li, Erik, and the campus security officer looked on. From what she could tell, the lock hadn't been jimmied or broken. There were no scratches on the tumbler, and the lock still turned easily when she tried to open it, using Li's key. "Whoever broke in either had a key to this room or a master."

"Only the police and the janitorial service have a master key," the officer told Nancy.

"Is it possible to gain access to the master keys, even for a moment?" Nancy asked, standing up.

The officer scratched his head. "Not in our office. The janitorial crew is another matter. I know they keep the keys locked up, but there isn't always someone in that office. I suppose someone could break in at night and steal a master key from them."

Nancy sighed. "What's your usual procedure on break-ins?" she asked the officer. "I know I'd like to have the penknife and door dusted for fingerprints."

"No can do," the officer replied. "We don't have the resources. You'd have to go to SFPD for that kind of thing. If you want my honest opinion, this is a prank."

Nancy knew that the last thing Wendy Kim would want would be to involve the San Francisco Police Department. She'd have to proceed on her own.

"Thanks," she said to the officer.

As soon as he was gone, both Li and Erik pounced on Nancy. "Of course this wasn't a prank," Erik said. "This is serious stuff. Why did you let him go like that?"

Nancy held up her hands in defense. "I wasn't going to convince him, and Soong's uncle doesn't want the police brought in."

Erik let out a long sigh, and once again Nancy wondered if this was all a big act. If so, Erik belonged on the stage, but not as a violinist.

Li held back her tears and said she could understand. "You did what you had to," she said. "But how will we ever find out who did this? And how do we know this kind of thing won't happen again?"

"We don't," Nancy said, aware that they were at even more of a dead end than Li suspected. Someone was following Soong and doing his best to undermine her confidence and peace of mind. That person could also try to kidnap her at any moment. Nancy's frustration was mounting, but there was nothing she could do except try to keep her cool and stay alert.

Erik packed up Soong's violin and went to retrieve his bow for her to use. He knew Soong's spare was being repaired. Li decided to stay behind and do some studying. Ten minutes later

Nancy and Erik were heading back to Hammond Hall. There, a worried Soong An greeted them in the lobby.

"Where have you been?" she asked. "My rehearsal's in less than ten minutes. I was worried you weren't going to make it."

By the expressions on their faces, Soong must have sensed that whatever had delayed them was important. "What's wrong?" she asked.

"Soong—" Erik gently took his hand in hers.

"Something terrible's happened!" Soong said with a wail. "Tell me. Did someone steal my violin?"

Soong's cries had caught the attention of several people, including George, and a tall man Nancy didn't recognize. The man had on a brown leather jacket and wore his long, brown hair tied back in a ponytail.

"What's going on, Erik?" the man asked, frowning at him from under his dark brows.

"I've got your violin right here," Nancy said, handing the case to Soong. Then, calmly and gently, Nancy explained what had happened to the bow. She didn't tell her about the note, however. She decided to wait until after Soong's rehearsal.

"I brought you my bow to use until you get yours fixed," Erik said to Soong.

A pained expression crossed Soong's dark eyes. "Is this another way to torment me?" Soong asked Nancy. "Will they not only go after me, but my music?"

"I hope not," said Nancy.

Soong sighed. "I must try to put all this aside and concentrate on my rehearsal."

"I'll go backstage with you," Nancy said firmly, aware that she shouldn't let Soong out of her sight.

"No!" Soong said, asserting herself. "No one but the performers are allowed backstage. There's a guard to make sure. I will be fine." With those words she strode into the concert hall.

Nancy watched her walk down the aisle. "I hope she can focus on her playing," Nancy said.

George gave a snort of laughter. "With that kind of determination," she said, "Soong will be fine."

Meanwhile, the man in the leather jacket and ponytail had taken Erik aside. "Smart move, Erik. You had an advantage over her, and you blew it."

"That's nice, Miles," Erik countered. "I want to win as much as you want me to, but I wasn't going to let Soong down. I had to lend her my bow."

"Who's that?" George asked Nancy.

"It must be Erik's manager," Nancy guessed. "Isn't his name Miles?"

"This was a lucky break," Miles was telling Erik. "Soong would have been out of the competition, and you would have had a terrific chance of winning."

Erik stared Miles down. "That's not how I want to win."

Miles threw his hands into the air. "Fine. Let's just hope nothing happens to that bow. I'll see you tomorrow, Erik. Make sure you get plenty of rest, okay? You look incredibly stressed, and that's not going to make for a very good performance."

As soon as Miles left, Erik muttered after him, "No kidding." Then he gave Nancy and George a glum look. "See you inside," he said. "Soong should be on pretty soon."

"We'll be right in," Nancy said. She had been keeping an eye on the stage, but she hung back, wanting to talk to George.

"It looks like all this pressure is getting to Erik," George said.

"You don't know the half of it," Nancy said. She told George about finding Erik with Soong's ruined bow in his hands.

George's brown eyes widened. "You don't think he did it, do you?"

"It's possible." Nancy thought for a moment, as the strains of the orchestra warming up filtered out to the lobby. "But if he did, why lend Soong his bow as a replacement?"

"Maybe he did it and then felt really guilty afterward?" George suggested.

"Maybe," Nancy agreed. Then she remembered the note and told George about that, too. "It's so confusing."

"I see what you mean," George said. "Tim An's enemies could do something a lot worse than ruin Soong's bow. On the other hand who else would try to harass Soong by leaving that note? And why? And what about the kidnapping threats?"

Nancy sighed. "So many questions—and no answers." From the lobby, she saw Soong walk onstage. "Soong's about to start," she said. "Let's grab some seats. We can keep our eyes on Soong, and maybe enjoy ourselves at the same time."

Frank and Joe Hardy were busy prowling the medical lab building, looking for the young man they believed to be Jeff Trask. So far, they'd searched the third and second floors and hadn't seen a sign of him. Now, they were on the first floor. They'd just turned the corner past Dr. Grossman's office, when Joe spotted the guy they had pulled from the lab. He was standing at the end of the hall talking to someone. Joe pushed Frank back against the wall.

"There he is," Joe whispered. "And look. He's talking to Stan."

Sure enough, Jeff and Stan were deep in conversation. The Hardys strained to listen to what the two guys were saying. Joe heard Stan say, "Listen, Jeff—" He couldn't make out the rest of the sentence, but he had heard enough. "That's our guy," Joe said quietly.

Stan and Jeff stood talking in the hall for another minute or two and then headed toward an open door off the hallway. They went into the room and closed the door behind them.

"Let's find out what they're doing," Frank said. He led the way down the hall, stopping at the room Jeff and Stan had disappeared into. It was a lab. Through the door's glass window, Joe spotted Jeff and Stan standing next to a workbench.

"What's he doing?" Frank asked over Joe's shoulder.

Joe reported the action to Frank. "Jeff's got a test tube, and he's adding some liquids to it. Stan's watching."

Stan had a wide smile on his face as Jeff worked. Jeff lit a Bunsen burner. Then he held the test tube over the burner.

"I think they're setting off another explosion!" Joe announced. He ducked away from the window. "I say we get out of here, fast."

Frank grabbed his brother's arm. "I'm not leaving until I catch one—or both—of them in the act."

Just then Joe heard a strange sound, as if a huge truck were rumbling by. Then the windows started shaking, and the ground beneath his feet rolled.

He grabbed onto the wall for balance, but the wall was vibrating. "What's going on?" Joe asked. His voice was shaking. The whole building was moving, and the noise had grown to a roar.

"I'm not positive," Frank said. "But it feels like we're having an earthquake."

Chapter

Ten

"N O WAY!" Joe Hardy cried, his eyes lighting with excitement. "I've never been in an earthquake before."

Frank Hardy wasn't excited, though. He felt as if he were on a ship, the floor vibrating and moving. He put his hand out to support himself on a wall and could feel the wall moving.

He looked into the lab and watched as Jeff lost his balance. The test tube in his hand hit the Bunsen burner and exploded into fire. Jeff and Stan flew back from it, then raced toward the door.

"Let's get out of here!" Frank warned. "They're on their way out. I don't want Stan to spot us."

He pulled Joe into the lab across the hall, just before Jeff and Stan had a chance to see them. The two men rushed down the hall as everything continued to sway and shake for a few moments longer.

"That nearly blew our cover," Frank said, his heart racing. "If Stan had seen us spying on him and Jeff, we would have had some quick explaining to do."

"The question is, what were they doing in that lab?" Joe asked.

"Let's find out," Frank said.

Frank and Joe left the lab they'd hidden in to discover a pile of debris in the hall. Parts of the dropped ceiling had fallen, revealing the fluorescent lighting tubes underneath. Inside the other lab the fire from the test tube had spread to a notebook near the Bunsen burner, and the smoke detector was blaring.

"Come on!" Frank cried, hurrying for a nearby fire extinguisher.

For the second time that day Frank and Joe fought a fire. By the time the firefighters arrived, Joe and Frank had the flames under control and were able to think about notifying Dean Harper of what they'd seen.

All up and down the medical labs, people were assessing damage, putting books back on shelves, and cleaning up broken glass. Frank and Joe ran into Dr. Grossman in the hall, and she gave them permission to use her phone. Frank put in his call to the dean.

"Two of our prime Ethics Now suspects were inside a lab when the 'quake hit," Frank told the dean on the phone. "We don't know if they intended to have this turn into an attack or if they were planning something else, but there was a small fire, which we got under control a few minutes ago."

Dean Harper let out a long sigh. "This earthquake has caused damage all over campus. I've sent my assistant, Mike Clark, over to check out the medical labs."

"Did you tell him about us?" Frank asked.

"Well, no," said the dean, a puzzled tone in his voice. "I didn't even know you boys were over there. Should I tell him when he gets back?"

"I think it's better if you don't," said Frank. "We thought about it, and we don't want anyone to know. We want to be completely undercover on this case. You should be the only one who knows what we're doing here, and why."

"I understand," said Dean Harper. "Meanwhile, I'm glad you boys have some suspects. Do you want to tell me more?"

Frank paused. "If you don't mind, I'd rather talk to you in person after we have some definite evidence. We'll keep you posted, don't worry."

Out of the corner of his eye, Frank saw Joe, who had been standing at the lab door, motioning to him. "Frank!" Joe whispered. "We've got to get out of here—fast."

Frank quickly said goodbye to Dean Harper. "What's up?" Frank asked.

"Peek out this window into the hall," Joe said. Frank looked out at the hallway. "Oh, man, I don't believe this," Frank said.

The gray-haired man who'd been in charge of the Ethics Now meeting was standing outside the lab, talking to Dr. Grossman.

Frank and Joe drew away from the door. "Well, we can't go out there, that's for sure," Frank said. "We'd better hide in Dr. Grossman's office and hope they don't come in here."

Frank and Joe just made it to the office as the door opened. "I'm so glad Dean Harper sent you over, Mike," Dr. Grossman said. "Look at this mess. It's going to take days to clean it up. How did the rest of the university hold up?"

From inside the medical lab director's office, Frank got a good look at the guy. There was no mistaking the graying hair, the glasses, and the dimple in the man's chin. Mike was definitely the Ethics Now coleader—and he was also Dean Harper's assistant.

"What are we going to do?" Joe whispered, peering over Frank's shoulder. "If they come in here, Mike's sure to recognize us. And Dr. Grossman knows we were asking about the attacks. What a mess."

On the other side of Dr. Grossman's office,

Frank spotted an open window. "We're going out that way," he said, nodding at the window.

Frank stepped over to the window and saw that it opened out onto an alley that ran along the med lab's basement. The drop was about ten feet.

"Not bad," he said. "As long as we hit the grass strip along the alley." He quickly climbed over the window ledge, counted to three, and fell. "Yikes!" he cried, barely landing on his feet with a jolt to his knees. "That was farther than I thought."

"Don't tell me," Joe said. "Here goes nothing."

Joe also landed on his feet. "We'd better take off before Dr. Grossman wonders why we left without saying goodbye."

"And how we managed to leave without her knowing it," Frank added with a grin.

Frank and Joe headed back to the dorm. On the way over, they saw more damage from the earthquake. Some of the university buildings had broken windows, and there were even some cracks in the brick faces.

"That was a lot of shaking, but I didn't realize it could cause so much damage," Joe said as they passed a building that had lost its chimney. "Somebody could have gotten seriously hurt if that thing fell on them."

"No kidding," Frank said. "We're just lucky that fire Jeff and Stan set off didn't cause any more damage than it did."

Once the Hardys got to the dorm, there was just time to shower and change before they had to meet Nancy, Soong, and George at Fisherman's Wharf. Both Hardys still felt a bit rattled from the earthquake, but they agreed that all the adrenaline pumping through their system had made them work up appetites.

Their suite had its own bathroom, which was lucky. That way Frank and Joe didn't have to worry about running into people on their floor. While Frank got dressed, Joe talked to him from the shower.

"So it looks like Stan and Jeff are our guys," Joe called out.

"Don't forget Mike Clark," Frank added as he adjusted his tie. He was wearing a denim shirt and chinos and decided to put on a brightly colored tie. He stood back from the mirror, combed his dark hair one last time, and decided he looked pretty good.

Joe appeared at the bathroom door with a towel wrapped around his waist. "Any reason for the tie?"

"I just wanted to look nice," said Frank.

"Not because of someone named Soong by any chance?" Joe pressed.

"No." Frank felt his face redden. "Well, maybe. I guess I do want to impress her. I don't know why, Joe, but I really like this girl."

"I can tell," Joe said. He had pulled on his

jeans and was reaching for a shirt in the closet. "I'm sort of surprised, to tell you the truth."

"Why?" Frank protested. "Soong's beautiful, and intelligent, and talented."

"And have you noticed how many guys turn to look at her when she walks by?" Joe asked.

"I know," Frank said, taking a last look in the mirror. "Do I stand a chance?"

"You're better looking than Erik," Joe said. "But you don't play the violin."

"I could learn!" Frank joked. "How long could it take?"

"Seriously, Frank," Joe said as he tucked in his shirt, "Soong will either like you for who you are, or she won't."

Frank snorted. "Did you read that in a magazine or something? Remind me to cancel your subscriptions."

The Hardys took a cab to Fisherman's Wharf. On the way over, Frank and Joe discussed the case a bit more. "Dean Harper's going to be upset to find out that his trusted assistant has been setting up attacks against the university," said Joe.

"We don't know that for sure," Frank said. "We know he's a member of the group and that he's doing it secretly or Dean Harper would have told us. But now that we do know who Mike is and where he works, it will be easier to do some serious investigating."

"I like the sound of that," Joe said. "What did you have in mind?"

Frank considered their options. "We can stake out the administration building and watch Mike during the day. Or—"

"Or we sneak into his office at night," Joe said, lowering his voice. "And see what we find in his desk."

"Now there's an idea," Frank agreed. "We might get a good lead by doing just that."

"Let's go for it," said Joe. "I brought my trusty tool kit, and you know which one I mean."

"My brother the lock picker!" Frank said. "Okay, it's risky, but let's do it. Tonight, after dinner."

The sun had begun to set on the bay, and the sky had taken on a beautiful, golden glow. Frank found his mind wandering from the mystery to a certain girl and what she might feel like in his arms. Of course, that would never happen, and he probably shouldn't even think about it, or about what her lips might feel like . . .

"Earth to Frank," said Joe. "We're here. Do you want to pay the man and get out, or would you like to sit here and stare at the back of his neck all night long?"

"Pay me, please," the cab driver said, smiling. "My neck isn't that pretty."

Frank got out of the cab and paid the driver. Joe pointed out Soong and George standing by the pier, feeding the sea gulls.

"Hey!" he called out. "How's it going?"

Frank held back for a moment, taking an extra second to watch Soong from a distance. Her long hair blew in the wind, and in her flowing skirt, she seemed almost to float beside Nancy and George. Joe was already on the pier, and Frank had to race to catch up.

"Hi, everyone!" Frank said. Although he greeted them all, his eyes searched out Soong's.

"Hi, Frank," Soong said, giving him a dazzling smile. "What about that earthquake, huh?"

"Where were you guys when it happened?" Joe asked. "Wasn't it wild?"

At the wharf, the damage from the 'quake seemed to be minor. A few windows were broken, but most of the restaurants were open for business, and the earthquake hadn't stopped the crowds.

"It sure was," George agreed. "Soong had just finished with her rehearsal. The chandelier in the concert hall started rattling, and the walls were shaking, and everyone ran for a doorway. I guess that's what you're supposed to do."

"Everyone ran for a doorway except George, that is," Nancy said, rolling her eyes in mock exasperation. "George just sat in her chair, laughing the whole time. I guess earthquakes bring out the weirdness in people."

"They must," Soong said. She shivered noticeably. "This has been the most stressful day, but I hope you're all hungry, because I know this place on the wharf that makes the best soft-shell crab sandwiches."

"I love soft-shell crabs!" Frank announced. Already he was under the spell of that strange, warm glow that came over him whenever he was around Soong. Nancy, George, and Joe went on ahead as Frank fell into step beside the violinist. The bay was on one side of Frank, and Soong was on the other, and while he walked with her, Frank found himself drinking in her beautiful high cheekbones, her lovely mouth, her dark, wide-set eyes.

He was so busy looking at Soong that Frank didn't hear his brother call out to him—until it was too late.

"Frank!" Joe warned. "Look out."

Frank stumbled over a box that was lying on the pier and reached out to grab the railing for balance. The railing gave way, and there was nothing between Frank and the cold waters of San Francisco Bay.

Chapter

Eleven

FRANK WOBBLED precariously on the very edge of the pier, his arms doing frantic windmills as he tried to keep from falling into the water below.

Joe lunged past Soong and grabbed onto his older brother's shirt. "Just in time," he announced, yanking his brother back onto the solid pier. "You were almost fish food."

Nancy, George, and Soong stood by, barely hiding their laughter. Joe could tell that Frank was embarrassed. "Don't worry," he told his older brother under his breath, "she'll never remember, not in a million years."

"Yeah, right," said Frank, staring down at the pier while the girls walked on ahead. "From now on, she'll never think of me as anything more than the guy who almost fell for her—literally." Frank gazed at Soong with longing.

Privately, Joe thought that Soong was the kind of girl a lot of guys fell for, and she probably let them all think they had a chance, even when they didn't. He didn't want to bring his brother down, so he said, "Just try to be more graceful in the future. And watch where you're going, okay?"

Frank and Joe caught up with the girls at the wharfside restaurant Soong had mentioned. It was on a pier that jutted out into the bay, and its tables were covered with red- and white-checkered tablecloths. There were white lights strung along the railings and red candles on the tables. The sunset had faded to dusk, and the glow from the candles and lights was warm and festive.

"I can't wait to dig into a plate of crab cakes and some hot chowder," George said.

The maitre d' sat them at a bayside table. Gulls swooped down, calling to one another and fighting for the scraps of bread that nearby diners tossed to them. Joe noticed that there were piers all along the wharf. Some of them had restaurants on them, while others were just for walking, fishing, or both. At the next pier over, Joe spotted couples strolling while fishermen packed up their gear. Joe was sitting next to Frank with Soong beside him. Across from them were Nancy and George. The busboy brought over their water, and a basket of piping hot sourdough bread. The waitress came to take their orders. Afterward, Nancy was buttering a slice of bread, when she suddenly stopped and pointed at the pier behind him.

"George, look!" Nancy announced. "There's that same guy I told you I saw talking to April earlier. I swear it's him, and he's been watching us," Nancy said. George looked in the direction Nancy was pointing and saw a guy running from the pier toward the wharf. "It's too dark," George said, squinting. "And he's got his back to me."

By now, Frank, Soong, and Joe had turned in their seats and were also gazing in the direction Nancy had pointed. "Who was he?" Frank asked.

Nancy frowned. "I wish I knew. Did anyone get a look at him?"

Soong shook her head, as did Joe.

"You want to tell us what's going on, Drew?" Joe asked. "I can see the wheels turning, but I don't have the vaguest idea what road you're on."

Nancy laughed. "I forgot. You guys aren't mind readers."

"Not yet," said Frank. "We're working on it though."

Joe listened as Nancy shared with them her suspicions about Soong's chaperon, April Jost. When Nancy got to the part about having seen April talking to a young man earlier that day at the concert hall, Soong interrupted.

"Can you describe the man?" she asked.

Nancy remembered that he was tall and had wavy, jet black hair. "He's from Philonesia. April said he was a relative of hers."

Soong drew in a deep breath but said nothing.

"Does this guy sound familiar?" Joe asked her.

"No," she said quickly. "Not at all."

"But your uncle knows April could still be dangerous," Frank put in.

"*Could* be," Soong emphasized. "For now, Uncle Tim knows that I feel very close to April. I was once quite attached to her other nephew, Jeffrey." Soong paused and hung her head. "We were in love, to tell the truth. But because Jeffrey's brother was Rupert Tran, my uncle forced us apart."

Soong stared off into the distance, her eyes were full of hurt and longing. Joe saw right then that no guy stood a chance with Soong. She was clearly still in love with this Jeffrey.

Soong turned back to Nancy and said, "Having April around reminds me of Jeffrey. I don't believe April would do anything to me, or to my uncle."

"But isn't it possible that Rupert might use her to get to you?" Joe wondered aloud.

"No," Soong insisted. "You must believe me when I tell you that April is above all this."

The waitress came with their dinners, putting a momentary stop to their conversation. By the time they were served, the group had forgotten about April, and Rupert, and the political situation in far-off Philonesia.

"This is incredible!" Frank said, taking a big bite of his soft-shell crab sandwich.

Joe dug into a crab cake. The patty was sweet and flavorful, with a spicy kick. "You're not kidding," Joe said. "And I usually don't even like fish."

As they ate, Nancy, George, Frank, and Joe asked Soong more questions about the competition. Soong entertained them with gossip and stories about her training, the pressure, her biggest fears. By the time dinner was over, Joe found himself won over by Soong's charm. The girl was just like any other nineteen-year-old—the only difference was that she was talented, beautiful, and from a foreign country. No wonder Frank was hooked. If Soong did put on airs, Joe understood how the life she'd led could make her a little spoiled. He decided not to hold it against her.

"Who's for dessert?" the waitress asked with a smile as she cleared their plates.

They all protested. Joe held his hands to his stomach. "I'm stuffed," he said. "I couldn't eat another bite."

Frank Hardy asked for the check. By the time they were dividing up the bill, Joe's mind was already on Mike Clark, and what he and Frank might learn when they searched his desk. Jeff was probably their number one suspect since he was around after each one of them, but the Hardys didn't have proof linking him to Ethics Now—except for having seen him with Stan. Mike Clark, however, was clearly important in the group. Yet he knew, better than anyone, how cooperative the university was being in banning animal testing.

Outside the restaurant was a crowd of people walking up and down Fisherman's Wharf. Nancy, Soong, and George wanted to join the Friday night buzz, but Joe reminded his brother about what they had planned.

"You want to let us in on what you're doing?" Nancy asked, smiling. "Or are you going to remain mysterious?"

Joe gave her a quick hug. "Now, if we told you, we'd have to tell everyone, right?" he asked. "See ya, Drew. Come on, Frank."

Frank said goodbye to Soong, then waved to George and Nancy. "Let's have breakfast tomorrow," he called out. "Nine o'clock, in the dining hall."

As they were hailing a cab to take them back to the university, Joe shook his head in disbelief. "I see why you've got a thing for Soong," he told his brother, "but just don't let it get to you, okay?"

"Why not?" Frank asked.

"She seems like she's still in love with this Jeffrey, don't you think?" Joe asked.

A yellow cab pulled to a halt in front of them. The Hardys got inside and gave the driver directions. Once they were under way and the driver was negotiating the heavy traffic out of Fisherman's Wharf, Frank answered his brother.

"I know you're right," he said with a sigh. "But I can't help how I feel."

Joe settled into the seat and stared out the window as the city went by. It really was a busy Friday night. The outdoor tables in front of streetside cafés were packed, and the sidewalks were full of people. He turned to look at his brother again, but when he saw the earnest expression on his face, Joe couldn't bring himself to pull Frank's feet back to solid ground. He'll just have to learn for himself, Joe thought. And if that means getting hurt, then he'll just have to get hurt.

Except for some outdoor floodlights, the administration building was dark when the Hardys arrived there ten minutes later. Rather than risk getting caught by entering through the main door, Frank and Joe searched out an entrance around the side. They quickly found a door that Joe was able to jimmy using his lock picking tool.

"Bingo," he said. The lock clicked, and Joe pushed the door open. "After you."

Frank stepped inside the dark hallway and turned on the flashlight he was carrying. Joe followed with his own flashlight. "This way," Joe said, leading them toward Dean Harper's office.

"Be careful," Frank warned in a whisper. "A

guard might come by, or someone could be working late."

The door to Dean Harper's office wasn't open, and Joe cringed a bit at having to pick the lock. "Let's hope Dad doesn't find out about this," he said under his breath. "I doubt he thought we'd come out here to spy on his own friend."

"We're not spying on Dean Harper," Frank reminded him.

"True enough," said Joe, "but we haven't told him we suspect his trusty assistant either."

In Dean Harper's outer office, Mike Clark's desk was its usual mess.

"That's a relief," Joe said, scanning the pile of papers. "There's so much clutter here, I can't see how he'd know we searched through his stuff."

"Watch out," Frank said with a laugh. "The messy ones always have some kind of weird filing system."

While Joe tackled Mike's desk, Frank started through the file cabinets next to it. Joe knew they had to find something that proved Mike gave the orders for Ethics Now or had committed one of the acts of sabotage. Or they had to find something that would explain his involvement in the group. But what were the chances that Mike would keep anything like that in his desk at work?

Almost all the papers on Mike's desk seemed to relate to his job as Dean Harper's assistant. There were budget reports, student evaluations, and course syllabuses. There were messages for the dean and for Mike, but Joe couldn't find anything that would link him to Stan or any other member of the group they'd met. There certainly wasn't anything like a list of planned actions against the university.

"Hold on," said Frank. Standing at the file cabinet, the older Hardy let out a long whistle. "Wow. I think we hit pay dirt."

"What is it?" Joe asked. He stood up and joined Frank at the file cabinets. Frank handed Joe a piece of paper. It was a letter from the university, addressed to Mike Clark. Skimming it quickly, Joe tried to make sense of what he read.

"This is a letter firing Mike as a faculty member," Joe said, confused. "So what's he doing working as Dean Harper's assistant?"

Frank took the letter back from Joe. "Good question. According to this, Mike used to be an assistant professor of molecular biology, but he was let go last semester when the university had to make tough budget cuts."

Joe thought for a moment. "If Mike Clark was fired, that gives him a big motive for wanting to get back at the university, right? Even stronger than being a thoroughly committed activist."

Frank had to agree. "You bet. And it means he has a special motive for targeting the medical labs. That's probably where he worked and taught. No wonder Dean Harper sent him over there today after the earthquake. Mike has a pretty good knowledge of what goes on in the labs and what would need to be repaired first after a 'quake."

Joe sat back down behind Mike Clark's desk, and shook his head—at the mess, and at the possibility that Clark was acting out a grudge against the university. "Why would he agree to work as Dean Harper's assistant? Do you think that all along he wanted to get even and that he took this job to make his revenge easier?"

"I don't know—" Frank stopped talking, when they both heard a sound in the hall outside Dean Harper's office.

"Quick," Joe cried. "Hide."

He was about to scoot under Mike Clark's desk, when suddenly the door opened, the lights went on, and the Hardys saw a familiar figure standing in the doorway.

It was Dean Harper himself.

Chapter

Twelve

FRANK," the dean cried out in surprise. "Joe! What are you boys doing here?"

Joe Hardy, who was halfway under Mike Clark's desk, awkwardly stood up while Frank quickly went to shut the file drawer. He held the paper in his hands behind his back and desperately tried to think of a way to get them out of this situation. There didn't seem to be any choice, except to come clean.

"The truth is," Frank said, "we were, uh—actually, we were snooping—" Frank cringed at the word. The dean didn't seem too happy to hear it either. "On Mike. On your assistant."

"You were spying on Mike Clark?" the dean demanded, his voice booming in the dark room. "Why on earth . . . ?"

"We have reason to think Mike Clark may be behind the attacks on the medical labs," Joe said.

Dean Harper looked back and forth between Frank and Joe, the confusion on his face evident. "You're going to have to explain this one, boys," he said angrily. "I trust Mike implicitly. I have no reason to think he'd betray that trust."

"Mike belongs to Ethics Now," Frank said quietly. "He was one of two people running the meeting we attended today."

"So you decided to invade his privacy—" the dean began.

"We couldn't say anything to you," Joe said. "Not until we had some kind of proof."

"And do you have that proof now?" Dean Harper demanded.

Frank showed the paper in his hand to the dean. "Actually, we think we do. According to this letter, Mike Clark was let go from his position as assistant professor during budget cutbacks."

"I know all about that," said the dean. "He took the job as my assistant because he didn't want to leave San Francisco. His wife has a good job, and their kids are in school here. We're hoping there will be enough money in the budget to rehire him next year."

From the testy tone in Dean Harper's voice, Frank could tell the man didn't want to think his assistant could be behind the attacks. Still, Frank felt it was important to make the dean see that their theory had some merit.

"Isn't it possible that Mike Clark wants to take revenge against the university?"

"It's possible," said the dean. "Even when Mike was an assistant professor, he was an outspoken critic of animal testing."

"The attacks started this semester, right?" said Joe.

"Yes," the dean agreed.

"When was Mike let go from his job?" Joe asked.

"Fall term was his last semester," the dean admitted reluctantly. "But I really think you've got the wrong man."

"Let's hope so," said Frank. He put the letter he'd found back in Mike Clark's file cabinet, then apologized to Dean Harper. "Joe and I should have been honest with you in the first place," Frank added. "I'm sorry we weren't."

"It's true we would have avoided this encounter," the dean agreed. For the first time that evening, he smiled. "Listen. From now on, let me know what you're up to, okay? Even— and especially—if it involves Mike. I'm very doubtful that he's the culprit here, but if that turns out to be true, I want to be the first to know."

"No problem," Joe said. There was an awkward moment, then Joe grinned and asked Dean

Harper, "So, do we leave the way we came in, or what?"

The next morning Nancy, George, and Soong were all up early. The Young Performers competition was a two-day event and would begin that morning. Soong wanted to divide her time between some last-minute practicing and watching the other competitors. Erik was to perform that day, but she wasn't on until Sunday. When he showed up at Soong's door that morning, Nancy noticed that his face was pale, and his eyes had dark circles under them.

"What happened to you?" Soong asked as she let him in.

"I couldn't sleep," Erik said, rubbing his face. "All night long, whenever I drifted off, I had these terrible nightmares. Either I lost my violin, or the music disappeared from the page, or the orchestra couldn't accompany me because they were laughing too hard. It was awful."

Soong took Erik's arm and led him into her room. "They were just bad dreams," she said, trying to reassure him.

Nancy and George, who were sitting on the couch, exchanged a smile. "I guess Erik's nightmares aren't very funny if you think about what they mean, and all the pressure he must feel he's under," said Nancy.

"That's how it is when I'm in a race. I dream that I'm running and running but I get nowhere," said George. "It's only funny when it happens to someone else. When it happens to you, it's the worst."

Just then Li came out of her room, dressed and ready to hit the library. In her arms was a stack of books, her backpack on her shoulder.

"Is Erik here?" she asked. "I thought I heard his voice."

"He's in Soong's room," Nancy said.

"Oh." Li's face fell. "Well, tell him I'll see him at the concert hall. I can't wait."

"Don't you want to have breakfast with us?" George asked. "We're leaving in a few minutes."

"No, thanks," Li said brightly. "I've got to do some serious cramming for my bio test. See you later."

Nancy and George took turns showering. Within twenty minutes, they were dressed and ready. Nancy had on a white T-shirt, red cardigan, blue jeans, and comfortable flats, while George was dressed in a black turtleneck, khakis, and running shoes. Erik had returned to his room to pick up his violin. Soong emerged from her bedroom a short time later wearing a flowing, silky skirt, a flowered top, and chunky black shoes.

"Where's Charlene?" George asked.

"She always sleeps through breakfast on Saturdays," Soong said.

Just then the phone rang. Nancy answered it. "Hello?"

First there was only silence on the other end. Then Nancy heard a woman's voice whisper, "Tell Soong An the danger grows. Every day she stays in this country, her life is more and more at risk."

Before Nancy could say a word, the woman hung up. A shiver went up Nancy's spine. The threats were definitely escalating. This one almost sounded like a death threat.

Quietly Nancy replaced the receiver. "Whoever it was hung up," she announced to Soong, who was standing expectantly by the phone. "Wrong number, I guess."

Soong shrugged and went back into her room. As soon as she was out of earshot, Nancy shared with George what had really happened.

"There must be a way to find out who's calling Soong," Nancy said. She thought for a moment, then snapped her fingers. "I've got a plan."

"You do?" George asked.

"You bet." Nancy reached for the Yellow Pages under the phone and quickly found what she was looking for. "In Illinois there's a service called 'Star Six-Nine' that lets you dial back the number that just called you," Nancy explained, "even if the other person hangs up."

"Cool," said George. "You call the person back and find out who's hanging up on you. Bingo, no more crank calls."

Nancy got through to the telephone company,

and within a few minutes, she had found out that California did indeed have the service and that it had to be ordered. She put in an order for Soong's phone. The operator informed her that the service would go into effect that evening.

With a feeling of satisfaction, Nancy hung up the phone. "Whoever's been calling Soong will have a surprise the next time they hang up," she said. "Because we're going to call her right back."

Soong reemerged from her room. At the same time, Erik reappeared at the door to Soong's suite.

"I hope you're ready to go," he said with a weary smile, "because I desperately need to get some food before I pass out."

After a quick breakfast with Frank and Joe, Nancy and George spent the rest of the day looking after Soong. All three attended the morning round of the Young Performers competition, which was when Erik was scheduled to play. As soon as Erik took the stage, all his tiredness seemed to vanish, and he gave a moving and impressive performance. When it was over, half the audience stood to clap.

At lunch in the dining hall afterward, Erik retained his confidence. "Miles says I didn't do my best, but I told him I think he's wrong." With that, Erik picked up his tray before he'd even finished. "I'm too excited to eat. Watch out,

Soong An," he said, pointing a friendly finger in her direction. "You may have stiffer competition than you think."

Once Erik had gone, Soong An sighed. "Erik is so talented. He's got as good a chance as I do to win, and he knows it. I just wish he hadn't gone ahead and hired Miles to manage his career. That guy puts him under too much pressure. Erik should be enjoying all this."

Soong spent the afternoon practicing in a rehearsal room upstairs from the concert hall while Nancy and George kept watch. At dinner that night with Li, Erik, Frank, and Joe, Soong was quiet and reserved. Nancy watched the girl and thought that perhaps she was starting to get nervous about her performance the next day, but then she remembered that Tim An was arriving. Soong's uncle was coming to try to convince her to return to Philonesia, and the girl was probably subdued at the prospect. Nancy thought there must be a way to lighten Soong's spirits.

"Why don't we all go out tonight after dinner?" Nancy asked. "Nothing too late, Soong, since you have to perform tomorrow, but it might be fun to go to a club or something."

"I don't know," Soong said. "I thought I should practice a bit more."

"Don't be silly," Erik said. "You can't practice the night before you perform. Everyone knows that just makes you more nervous. I'm sure that's why I had those bad dreams last night."

"I'm sure that didn't make a difference," Li said. "Your performance was terrific."

Frank and Joe were up for a short evening out, and Soong finally warmed to the idea as well. She suggested they try out Groove, a new club that had opened in the downtown warehouse district. While the boys got ready, Nancy, Soong, and George went back to Soong's room to change. Li parted from the group, deciding on a night of studying in the library instead.

In Soong's suite, Charlene and her boyfriend, Stan, were hanging out in the living room, watching a movie on the VCR.

"What's up?" Charlene asked.

"We're going to Groove," Soong told her. "Want to come along?"

Stan wrapped his arms around Charlene and gave her a kiss on the ear. "No, thanks," he said. "I think we'll stay here and take advantage of the privacy. But have fun."

Before they left, Soong thought to call April at home and let her know they were all going out. "She is my chaperon, after all," Soong said. "I always let her know when I'm going off-campus." She left a message on April's answering machine.

"Have fun," Charlene called after them as they left.

Frank, Joe, and Erik were waiting in front of the dorm when the girls emerged. Rather than taking the cable car, the group decided to walk over to University Avenue and hail a couple of cabs. Erik and Soong got into the first cab that stopped. Soong told Nancy the address of the club.

"I'll stick with these guys," an eager Frank Hardy said, jumping into the front seat of the cab. "I can keep an eye on Soong while you guys follow us."

"Do you feel like we've been dumped?" Joe asked, watching the taillights of the cab disappear into traffic.

"Nah," George said. "Just left a little high and dry."

"If Frank wants to play bodyguard," said Nancy with a laugh, "then let him." She thought of how she'd spent all day tagging along with Soong. It wasn't exactly boring, but it hadn't been the most exciting twelve hours either. "He'll see it's not all fun and glamour."

"I don't think Frank cares too much about the guarding part," Joe said.

Another cab came along a moment later, and the trio piled inside. Nancy gave the driver the address Soong had given her. Soon they were passing the skyscrapers downtown. Then the driver headed for the warehouse district and the piers. Here, the streets were darker, and the sidewalks empty.

"Nice neighborhood," Joe said.

The driver pulled to a stop in front of a warehouse building where there was a neon sign that read Groove. Soong, Erik, and Frank were outside waiting.

Nancy stepped out of the cab and was just about to pay the fare when she heard a car screech to a halt in front of the club. Two men emerged from the car. They were wearing ski masks and had on dark clothes. Nancy's instincts went on red alert.

"Frank," Nancy cried. "Look out for Soong."

The men had already pushed past Frank and Erik and grabbed a surprised Soong.

"Help," the young violinist called out. "Somebody help."

Nancy watched as the men dragged Soong to their waiting car. This time Soong An was really going to be kidnapped.

Chapter

Thirteen

THE TWO MEN tried to push the struggling Soong An into their waiting car while Frank, Erik, and Joe sprang into action. Instantly a kidnapper pulled a revolver from a shoulder holster and trained it on them. The trio backed off, their hands raised high.

Nancy knew if she or George didn't act, the men would succeed in their kidnapping attempt.

Nancy tossed a ten-dollar bill at the cab driver, told George to stay put, and took off in a low crouch for the kidnapper's car. While the one man continued to train his gun on Joe, Erik, and Frank, the other man had pushed Soong into the backseat and was trying to close the door on her. She was kicking out at him furiously.

Moving quickly and quietly, Nancy took advantage of all the activity and sneaked up on the kidnapper who was still trying to push Soong's legs inside. Nancy delivered a swift karate blow to his shoulder, which was enough to stun him. As he fell against the side of the car, Nancy then whirled around and kicked the back of the gunman's knees—instantly he, too, collapsed.

"Come on," Nancy said to Soong, and reached for the girl's hand, pulling her to safety.

Frank, Erik, and Joe started to close in on the kidnappers, but the two men were already recovering from Nancy's blows. The gunman had picked himself up and was leveling his automatic pistol at them once more. The one slumped against the car was standing, ready to take Nancy on.

A crowd had started to form outside the club. "What's going on?" Nancy heard someone shout. "Who are these guys?"

The Hardys, Erik, George, and Nancy—with Soong hidden behind her—stood motionless in a tight circle around the car, ready to make a move if they got a chance.

"Five against two," Joe pointed out to the men. "Pretty bad odds."

The gunman shouted a single word in a foreign language, then brandished his gun. Soong's other attacker slowly opened the front passenger door and slid inside the car.

"Abunai!" the man with the gun warned. He gestured for them to back off. *"Abunai!"*

Joe held his hands in the air and backed away. The others did the same. Nancy watched in utter frustration as the man inside the car slid over into the driver's seat, started the engine, and called out to his cohort. The man with the gun hopped into the car and slammed the door. With a squeal of brakes, the driver took off.

Nancy watched the taillights disappear, then kicked the ground in frustration. "We had them," she said.

"But they had the gun," Frank pointed out.

"Did any of you get a look at the license plate?" Nancy asked her friends. "Maybe we can trace the car."

"I only got the first two numbers," George told her. "It was too dark."

Nancy's frustration grew. She knew that the first two numbers wouldn't give them very much, even with a description of the car—a late model, American made, dark blue sedan. Besides, Tim An didn't want to involve the police, and that's what they'd have to do if they wanted to trace the car. All Nancy knew at this point was that the kidnappers spoke a foreign language, which she had a pretty good idea was Philonesian. A rattled Soong An confirmed Nancy's suspicions.

"Yes," she said. "They were speaking Philonesian. *Abunai* means 'back off.'"

The crowd that had formed was slowly dispersing. Erik had his arm around Soong and was comforting her. Nancy's mind was spinning—how had the kidnappers found Soong this time.

"You called April to tell her where you were going, didn't you?" Nancy remembered.

"I did," said Soong, "but you are wrong about April. She wouldn't jeopardize her position in the consulate, or as someone my father trusts. Not even for a nephew."

"Who else knew where we were going?" Frank asked.

George counted off on her fingers. "Li, Charlene, her boyfriend. Anyone else?"

Nancy thought hard. "Not that I remember." In the distance, Nancy could hear the foghorns, and she became aware of the dense mist rolling in from the bay. As far as Nancy was concerned, their evening out was over, but Erik thought differently.

"Why don't we all go inside?" he suggested. "There's no point in letting those goons ruin our evening."

"I doubt Soong feels like dancing right now," George said sympathetically. "Do you?"

Soong gave them all a brave smile. "Maybe it would take my mind off *everything*"—she emphasized the word—"just to have a little fun."

"Let's do it then," Nancy agreed. "If nothing else, we'll be safer inside with all those people around."

The group spent the next few hours dancing

and talking. Even Nancy was able to forget, now and then, about the kidnappers. The club was decorated in funky, mismatched furniture. On the walls were posters for the latest bands and for marches and protests in support of local causes. The crowd was low-key, friendly, and relaxed.

Even with all the great music and dancing, Nancy kept thinking about the case and trying to piece together what she knew. April Jost had known about Soong's whereabouts both times she was almost kidnapped, and April still seemed to have the strongest motive for being involved in the attempts, despite everything that Soong said. That didn't solve the problem of who had ruined Soong's bow and why, or who left that doll for Soong. How did the ruined bow and the doll relate to the kidnapping? Also, Nancy still couldn't be sure that April was behind the threatening phone calls Soong had received.

Soon, she thought, as she sat at a table and sipped a soft drink, she'd have a real break in the case. The *69 service would be in effect that evening, so the next time Soong got a threatening call, they could ring the number back. In the meantime she had to continue to protect Soong.

"Earth to Nancy." She heard Joe Hardy's voice. "I'm only asking you to dance. You can say no if you want. You don't have to pretend I don't exist."

"Joe!" Nancy exclaimed. "I'm sorry. I didn't hear you."

Their table looked out on the dance floor. Nancy was sitting in an oversize armchair, while Joe was perched across from her on a stool. He took a long sip of his soda and said, "You want to tell me what's on your mind?"

"I was thinking about my case," Nancy said. "None of the facts are coming together for me."

"It's a tough case," Joe agreed.

Nancy smiled. It was always good to talk to someone who understood. Since she thought of Frank as her main friend, she sometimes forgot that she and Joe Hardy had a lot in common as well. She glanced at Joe and noticed that he seemed preoccupied as he watched Frank dance with Soong.

"What's the matter with you?" Nancy asked him. "Are you having trouble, too?"

Joe shrugged. "Our case is going okay, I guess. We've got a lead or two, but we're mostly just staking out our main suspects."

"Are you worried about Frank?" Nancy guessed, watching Joe eye his older brother.

"Maybe." Joe paused, then turned to Nancy, a perplexed expression on his face. "I don't get it, Nancy. Frank's always so cool with girls. And I know he really likes Callie, his girlfriend back home. But this time he really seems to have a thing for Soong, and I can't bring myself to tell him—"

"That he doesn't stand a chance," Nancy said, feeling a little twinge of jealousy now that they were talking about it. Yes, she had Ned back home, but the best part of hanging out with the Hardys was getting to spend time with Frank. So far that just hadn't happened. Watching him dance with Soong, Nancy saw the dreamy expression on his face, and she knew there was no way they could bring him back to earth.

"He'll have to find out the hard way," Nancy said.

"Yeah," Joe agreed glumly. He ran a hand through his blond hair and sighed. "But none of you has to live with him after she breaks his heart."

"I guess you're right," Nancy agreed with a smile. "You really do have the harder job."

For the next half hour Nancy and Joe talked while the others danced. Joe confided to Nancy a little bit about their case, and Nancy used Joe as a sounding board for her own mystery.

Finally a very tired Soong came back to the table, with Frank in tow. After George and Erik returned, the group decided to head back to the dorm.

"I don't want to be exhausted tomorrow," said Soong, "even though I'm having a terrific time."

Soong gave Frank Hardy a wide smile. Nancy noticed that Erik flinched. Maybe Joe and she were wrong, Nancy thought. Maybe Soong really could like Frank. It was possible. Still, when they got up to go, Soong walked ahead of the group with Erik, and the two were soon gossiping about the music world and discussing the competition. A dejected Frank Hardy walked behind them and Nancy found herself revising her opinion yet again: Soong An liked to flirt. She flitted from Frank to Erik, and didn't stop to think about how her behavior affected either one of them.

The girls split from the boys, and each group hailed a cab back to the dorms. It was after ten when Nancy, George, and Soong got back to Jarman.

"What a day!" George exclaimed, falling onto the couch in Soong's suite.

Charlene's door was shut, and so was Li's. Soong went to check the messages on the answering machine, and Nancy listened, too. She gave an involuntary gasp when she heard a woman's voice on the tape.

"There is no escape, Soong An. Perform tomorrow, and you are risking all."

Soong stood by the machine, stunned.

"It's the same woman who called before," Nancy said.

"The voice does sound the same," Soong agreed, finding her composure.

Nancy picked up the receiver. "Luckily, that was the last message." The answering machine had beeped a last time and was rewinding. "So we'll be able to trace it."

Soong seemed confused. Nancy explained to her about the call earlier that day and how she'd arranged for the callback feature. Now, she dialed *69, and waited as the phone rang. And rang. And rang.

"There's no answer," Nancy said, her disappointment rising. She counted to ten rings and was about to hang up. Just then, a man answered the phone.

"Hello?" the male voice asked, breathless.

Nancy was confused. She'd expected to reach the person who'd called Soong—and that person was a woman.

"Hello?" the voice repeated.

Beyond her confusion, Nancy found there was something strangely familiar about the voice, something she thought she recognized.

"Who is this?" the man demanded.

Finally Nancy was able to figure out why the voice sounded so familiar: The person on the other end of the line was Erik Kolker.

Chapter

Fourteen

ERIK SAID HELLO a fourth time as Nancy quietly hung up the phone.

"Nancy, who was it?" George asked. "You look like you've just heard a ghost."

"A ghost?" Nancy asked. "No. Just Erik Kolker."

"Erik!" George exclaimed. "But the voice on the answering machine has been a woman's."

"Exactly," Nancy said. She sat down and tried to make sense of what had just happened as Soong and George looked on.

"I don't understand," Soong said. "Erik isn't the one making these calls to me, is he?"

"I don't see how he could be," Nancy said. "At least not without an accomplice." She thought immediately about catching Erik with Soong's damaged bow. The threat on the machine just now was that if Soong performed, she'd risk everything. Erik could want to scare Soong so much that she wouldn't perform.

"I've wondered for a while if these phone calls aren't related to the kidnapping attempts," Nancy said, putting her thoughts together out loud.

"What do you mean?" George asked.

"The notes and calls—except for the first one, which we only heard about—tell Soong An to go home," Nancy pointed out. "If someone's trying to kidnap Soong, wouldn't they want her to stay here? And would they *warn* her that she's going to be kidnapped or that her life is in danger? It makes sense that her uncle got threats about Soong because the terrorists thought they could scare him into stepping down from the presidency. But if Soong is safely back in Philonesia, the terrorists would no longer have any leverage."

"I see what you mean," said George.

"I don't," Soong put in.

Nancy tried to explain, knowing it wouldn't be easy to make Soong face the fact that Erik could be responsible for the calls and the notes.

"What if Erik had a female friend call Soong to make threats—in the hope that the calls might force Soong out of the competition? It's possible that Erik took advantage of the original kidnapping threats to do his own form of harassment.

What if we've really got *two* mysteries instead of one?"

"Erik wouldn't threaten me," Soong stated flatly. "There's got to be a good explanation for why that call came from his room."

"I'm sorry, Soong, but I'm just trying to make sense of what we know," Nancy said, wishing she could be more gentle. "It's possible that the competition has really gotten to Erik. Maybe he was talked into this—"

"By Miles, you mean?" George asked.

"Could be," Nancy agreed. "There's still the question of who made the calls."

"What makes you so sure it's not the kidnapper?" Soong asked petulantly. "Doesn't that make the most sense?"

"How did the kidnapper—or some female accomplice, since the calls are from a woman—get into Erik's room?" Nancy wanted to know. "That's where we traced this call back to."

"You think Erik destroyed my bow, don't you?" Soong demanded.

Nancy was silent, and George stared down at the floor, unable to defend Erik.

Soong glared at Nancy, then at George. "You do, don't you?" She made a noise of disgust. "You're wrong, you're wrong! I just know it." With that, Soong An stormed into her bedroom and slammed the door shut.

"Yikes," said George, wincing. "Welcome

back the Soong An we know and love. Still, I can't blame her for being angry. Before, it was April who Soong didn't want us to suspect. Now it's Erik. She must think we really have it in for her."

Nancy let out a long sigh. "I guess I didn't handle that too well, huh?"

"Don't worry, Nan," George reassured her. "Your job is to protect Soong and figure out who's trying to kidnap her. You don't have to be best friends."

Nancy laughed. "I don't think there's any danger of that happening. Just when I think we're starting to understand each other, and maybe even like each other, something like this happens."

"She'll come around," said George. She started unfolding the sofa bed, but stopped midway. "You don't think Erik's working with April, do you?" George asked.

Nancy sighed and ran a hand through her hair. Soong's closed door still stung like a strong rebuke. "I don't know," she said. "We have to keep our eyes on Erik. All I know is that the last threatening call came from his phone."

"Even if *he* didn't make it," George said, stifling a yawn, "he might have a good idea of who did."

"Exactly," Nancy said, aware that they were no closer to understanding who was after Soong.

"Let's just hope we get a better idea before someone manages to nab Soong."

Joe Hardy awoke with a start. The phone on the nightstand beside his bed was ringing, but he saw that it was still dark outside. He fumbled for his watch and the receiver at the same time. According to his watch, it was five o'clock in the morning.

"Who is this?" Joe demanded, his voice hoarse.

In the bed across from him, Frank stirred, then sat up. "What's going on?" Frank asked sleepily. "Was that the phone?"

"This is your contact at Ethics Now," a man's voice on the other end said to Joe. "Who's this?"

"Joe Hardy." Joe motioned for Frank to quiet down.

"We have your assignment, Joe," the man said, his voice low and gruff. "You and your brother are to proceed to the medical labs. The main entrance will be left open for you. Go to lab five. In the lab's refrigerator you'll find animal protein specimens. They belong to Jeff Trask. They're in marked petri dishes. Dump the specimens in the sink."

"But that must be his research," Joe protested. "Can't we find something less—less vicious?"

"You don't have the option to choose a second assignment," the man snapped. "You are to leave a note by the sink that reads 'Stop animal testing, or we'll stop you' and sign it Ethics Now. Do you understand?"

"I understand," Joe said.

"And plan to attend a meeting in the basement of the student center at nine," the voice went on. "We want to make sure the action went as planned."

Joe let out a long sigh. Frank wasn't going to be happy about this one. They couldn't destroy research that might be invaluable. Since Joe didn't recognize the voice giving him the instructions, he knew they were no closer to figuring out who were the group's leaders. He simply wasn't sure it was Mike Clark, or even Stan. If Jeff himself was involved, why was the group having them destroy his own research?

"And, Joe?"

"Yes?"

"Don't think about not going ahead because we'll be there, watching to make sure you and your brother are on the up-and-up," the man said. "Get it?"

"I get it."

With that, Joe heard a click and then the dull hum of a dial tone. Frank looked over at Joe expectantly.

"Well?"

Joe relayed their assignment to his brother. "It's bad, Frank," Joe said. "You were right. We could do some real damage."

"We're not going to do it," Frank said.

"We don't have that option," said Joe. He explained how the caller had let him know that the Hardys would be watched, and that they were to attend a meeting at nine to confirm they'd gone ahead with the attack. Then a thought occurred to Joe. "In which case, we really should go ahead with the plan, because maybe we can outsneak them."

"What do you mean?" Frank asked.

"We'll scope out the scopers." Frank still looked sleepy and confused. "We'll lay a trap for them," Joe explained. "The only way they know that we've committed the action is if they come around to check up on us. We'll hide out in the lab and wait for whoever it is to show up. Then we'll know for sure who's involved."

"You're assuming that the person who gives the orders is also the person who will check up on us," Frank said. "What if that's not true?"

Joe rubbed his eyes in frustration. "Maybe it's not. But I can't think of any other way around this. Can you?"

"No," Frank agreed. "Okay. We'll go up to the labs and wait in lab five. After an hour or so, if no one comes along, we leave."

"What about the meeting?" Joe asked. "How will we explain why we didn't commit the action?"

"I don't know," said Frank in exasperation. "Maybe we'll tell the truth: that we decided it was too nasty to destroy the guy's research. Either they give us another assignment or not."

For the next few minutes Joe Hardy concentrated on getting ready—and waking up. Five o'clock in the morning wasn't prime time for him. After a hot shower, though, he felt more prepared for what they had to do.

The campus was deserted as Frank and Joe headed over to the medical labs. Hill Street was completely empty, and the sun was just coming up when Joe went to the front entrance of the medical labs building.

"It's open, all right," Joe said.

"That's something that bothers me," Frank said, digging his hands into the pockets of his jacket.

"What?" asked Joe.

"Whoever set us up for this must have a key," Frank said.

"Meaning Mike Clark," Joe said.

"Or Jeff himself," said Frank.

"I don't get it." Joe frowned. "Why would Jeff have us destroy his own research?"

"To make it seem like he wasn't responsible," said Frank. "Think about it. What better way to lay the blame on someone else? Right now, the suspicion points to Jeff. Maybe he wanted to make the trail cold again."

"But we don't even know for sure that Jeff belongs to Ethics Now," Joe said. "He wasn't at that meeting."

"No," Frank agreed. "But we did see him with Stan in the lab before the earthquake. And," Frank continued, "didn't Mike say that since Stan joined, the group had become more subversive? What if Stan and Jeff are working together?"

Joe held open the door for his brother. "It's something to think about," he said. "For now, let's get on with this action. I'm nervous about standing around outside."

Inside, the hallway was dark, except for dim night lights along the baseboards. "Keep an eye out for guests," Joe told his brother. "They could be watching us at any point."

Upstairs at lab five, the door was also open. In the dim light, Joe saw a sign on the door of the refrigerator across the room. He went over to it and read the note. It read Welcome.

Joe showed the sign to Frank and grimaced. He opened the refrigerator door and saw another sign, this one pointing to the animal protein samples in their petri dishes.

"'These are the ones,'" Joe read aloud. "Well, thanks. We'd probably be too stupid to figure that out." Joe reached inside the refrigerator and took out one of the samples. He was about to put it back when he heard footsteps in the hall outside.

"Get down," Joe warned his brother. "I think we've got company."

Frank ducked behind the bench, while Joe searched for a hiding spot. He was just crawling toward Frank, when a voice called out from a portable bullhorn.

"This is the police. Come out with your hands up. You're under arrest!"

Chapter

Fifteen

THE ROOM became flooded with light, and Frank heard the sound of half a dozen men rushing into the lab. "We've got a whole team here," the voice announced. "You won't get away!"

Great, Frank Hardy thought. Just great.

He stood up from behind the lab bench with his arms raised, only to discover he was being faced down by half a dozen officers from the San Francisco Police Department, all fully armed.

"We're not going to try anything funny," Frank said. "So would you mind putting those guns down?"

A lieutenant gave the order. "You can drop your weapons, men," he said, not bothering with his bullhorn.

Joe Hardy stood up, a stunned expression on his face. He held the animal protein sample in one hand. The other, Joe held aloft. When he saw Frank looking his way, Joe simply shrugged.

"Sorry," he said. "You were right."

The lieutenant had his men approach Frank and Joe. Before Frank knew what was happening, his hands were in cuffs, and he was being led out of the lab and the building, toward a waiting police car.

"You've got the wrong idea," he tried to tell the lieutenant. "Call Dean Harper, he'll explain everything."

"Right," said the lieutenant. He stood by the door to the cruiser as Joe and Frank were pushed into the backseat. "He'll be able to tell me why you boys were sneaking around the med labs at six in the morning. Maybe he'll even be able to tell me what you were planning to do with that lab sample you were holding when we got there, young man," the lieutenant added, addressing Joe.

"Nothing," said Joe. "Honest."

"Just looking, huh?" the lieutenant asked. "Then I guess you don't know anything about the sabotage that was about to go on in that lab, and you wouldn't be the two boys we were warned about. And it's just a coincidence that the lab sample you were holding is also the same one that was about to get tossed down the sink, huh?"

"What makes you say that?" Frank asked the lieutenant. "You seem to know a lot."

"Ten minutes ago we got a phone call tipping us off about what you boys were up to," the lieutenant explained.

Frank flinched. They'd been set up. Someone who knew about the action had decided to frame them for it. Maybe even the same guy who'd given Joe their orders. The question was—who and why?

"I'm telling you," Frank said. "You should call Dean Harper. He can straighten this all out."

"I'll let you call Dean Harper," said the lieutenant as he started to shut the door on Frank and Joe, "just as soon as we get you boys down to the station."

The police station was located just down the hill on University, a few blocks from the school itself. There, Frank and Joe put in a call to Dean Harper at home. He immediately offered to explain to the police lieutenant.

"You boys are having some bad luck, eh?" the dean said with a soft chuckle. "First I catch you, then the police do. Maybe I should call Fenton and have him give you a brushup on how to investigate without getting caught."

"I guess we deserve that," Frank said, wincing. "But right now, I just don't feel much like laughing."

"Don't worry," the dean reassured him. "I'll call the lieutenant and take care of everything."

The two officers guarding Frank and Joe led them to a small room where there was a couch and two chairs. Within a few minutes the lieutenant came into the room and told his men to unlock Frank and Joe's handcuffs.

"You're free to go," he said, obviously chagrined. "I just had a nice chat with Dean Harper. We decided this was all a big misunderstanding." The lieutenant wiped a hand across the top of his bald head. "Sorry, boys."

"No problem," said Frank. He rubbed his sore wrists and stood up. "Now that you realize we're telling the truth, I'd like to know more about who tipped you off."

"I didn't take the call," the lieutenant said. "My desk sergeant did. But he tells me that a woman called and reported that there would be two young men breaking into lab five and that they were planning to destroy some research specimens."

"A young woman?" Joe asked.

"That's what he tells me," the lieutenant said.

Frank could think of only one young woman they knew in Ethics Now: Charlene. He couldn't wait to get outside the station and talk over his suspicion with Joe. In the meantime, though, he knew they had to keep their cover intact. He asked the lieutenant to make it look as though he and Joe had been formally arrested and released. "Believe me, there's a reason."

The lieutenant shrugged and had his desk

sergeant formally book Frank and Joe on suspicion of sabotage. The charges could be dropped later, but for now the Hardys were fingerprinted and read their rights, then let go on their own recognizance.

"Nice going," said Joe, wiping the ink off his fingertips. "I feel like a professional crook, thanks to you."

"We needed to keep our cover," Frank reminded him. "Until we find out who tipped us off, it has to seem like we were really arrested."

The Hardys were standing in front of the police station. By the time they'd been fingerprinted and charged, they'd been in the station for almost two hours. It was past eight o'clock in the morning.

"We have time for a quick breakfast before that nine o'clock Ethics Now meeting," Frank said. He was beginning to feel the effects of having gotten up so early and not having eaten. "Let's head over to the dining hall to see if the others are there."

The Hardys walked up the hill toward the dining hall. Nancy, Soong, and George must not be up yet, Frank decided when he didn't see them. He tried to hide his disappointment, but Joe caught on. Once they were sitting down, Frank's brother couldn't resist a barb.

"Guess you'll have to think about the mystery for now. Your girlfriend's not up yet."

"Ouch," said Frank, wincing. "That one stung."

"The truth hurts, Frank," said Joe as he dug into his pancakes.

"You really think I've been letting our work slide?" Frank asked his brother.

"Only a few feet," replied Joe. "But I know you'll get back on track."

"Right." Frank swallowed some juice. To prove his mind really was on the case, he brought up his theory about Charlene with Joe. "If it really was a woman, who else could know about the attack except Charlene?" Frank asked his brother. "There are other women in the group, but I saw the hug she gave Stan at the end of the first meeting we went to. I got the feeling she's pretty tight with Stan, and we have good reason to suspect that Stan is one of the main Ethics Now leaders."

"Good thought," said Joe. "I take back what I said just now. I say we confront Charlene with what we know."

"Not yet," Frank warned. "We still need to know who gave the order and what the motives might be. If it was Stan, why is he obsessed with targeting only the university and not other organizations or businesses that are cruel to animals? If it's Mike, why would he jeopardize his getting rehired as a professor? Does he want revenge that badly?"

"Or is it someone else entirely?" Joe wondered aloud. "Someone we're not considering."

"Exactly," said Frank. "We have to keep our eyes and ears open, and make sure we don't blow our cover. But I think this lead about the female caller is the beginning of a real break for us."

The Hardys finished their breakfast and then headed over to the student center. In the basement, the Ethics Now meeting was just getting under way. This time, Paul and Charlene were leading the group. Obviously, the leadership changed on Sunday. Frank wondered if that meant their attack fell under Charlene and Paul's leadership. That would mean that Charlene knew enough about the attack to call the police.

All these questions, Frank thought as he took a seat in the circle.

Frank forced himself to stop thinking about the case as Charlene and Paul went over old business and then proceeded to ask Frank and Joe how their attack had gone.

"Just fine until the police showed up," said Joe.

"Dude, no way." Paul's blue eyes registered shock, and he leaned forward in his chair. "What happened?"

"They were tipped off," Frank said. He tried to catch Charlene's eye, but the young woman was taking notes on the pad in her lap.

"Bad news," Stan said. "Sounds like we've got a leak here."

"Don't be so quick to judge," Mike warned.

"If the police showed up, someone must have tipped them off," another young man said. "Did the cops tell you anything?"

"Nope," said Joe. "Not a word. They fingerprinted us, though." He held up his stained fingers. "And we have to show up for a hearing in a month."

"Major drag," said Paul. He kicked at the floor with his sneaker. "I agree with Stan. We've got a leak, and we need to find out who it is before we go any further."

Charlene stopped writing for a moment. She held her pen to her lips and then spoke up. "This is something we'll need to discuss with permanent members only," she said. Turning to Frank and Joe, she added, "I'm afraid we'll have to ask you to leave."

"No problem," Joe said.

The Hardys waited in the hall for a good fifteen minutes. Finally Stan came out and told them they were free to go. "This business about a possible leak is a big problem for the group," he said. "I'd hate to think that all our hard work is starting to unravel just because someone doesn't have the guts to follow through. Meanwhile, we'll be contacting you about another assignment." He put a hand on Frank's arm. "I'm sorry you didn't get to follow through on the one you had."

With that he went back into the meeting,

leaving Frank and Joe out. "Do you think they suspect us?" Joe asked.

Frank thought for a moment. "Who knows? I still have some questions I want to ask Mike Clark, though. Let's hang around until the meeting's over and see what he's willing to tell us."

Ten minutes later the door opened again, and the members of Ethics Now sauntered out. Charlene seemed rattled. She was talking to Stan, defending her leadership abilities, saying she was interested in animal rights above any procedural problem. Stan had his voice raised in disagreement. The pair left as Frank and Joe stepped back inside.

Frank thought that if Charlene had tipped off the police, Stan would be pretty upset to find that out. Frank had a feeling that Charlene, along with some other members, didn't like the direction in which the group was headed. Was her dislike strong enough to undermine Stan's orders? Frank made a mental note to ask Nancy more about Charlene. Maybe she had some insights into the girl's character. Maybe she even knew something about Stan.

Mike Clark was gathering up his belongings. When he saw that Frank and Joe had returned, he seemed surprised.

"Didn't Stan talk to you?" he asked.

"He did," said Frank, "but *we* wanted to talk to *you*."

"Sure," Mike said with a smile. "What about?"

"My brother and I are worried, to tell you the truth," Frank began.

"We're not sure this is really the group for us," said Joe.

"If it's about how you were caught by the police," Mike said, "I'm really sorry about that. We're doing our best to find out what happened."

"That's not all," Frank put in. "Some friends of ours here at SFU say we shouldn't join Ethics Now. They say that some members have personal grudges and that the group's motives and tactics aren't always pure."

Mike sighed and pushed his glasses up on his nose. "I know why they're saying that," he offered. "It's because I used to be an assistant professor, and they probably think I'm working out some grudge."

Frank was surprised that Mike was being so honest with them. "Are you?" he asked.

"No," Mike insisted. "I was against animal testing before my job was eliminated, and I'll be against it when they rehire me." He dug his hands into his jeans pockets and stared at both Hardys earnestly. "A few members of this group want to take things too far, I admit that. I'm not always in favor of the group's decisions, but I go along because I agree with them in principle. Personally, I'd like to see other targets besides the medical labs, especially since the administration *has* been cooperative, but Stan and some others want to keep the pressure on."

"I guess our friends were wrong about your motives then," said Frank. "I know we feel reassured about that."

Mike smiled, then shook the Hardys' hands. "Don't give up on us until you understand better what we're all about," he said. "There are a lot of different voices here, and we all want to be heard while staying focused on our goals."

Mike Clark walked out with the Hardys. On the way out of the student center, they passed a café. There Stan, Charlene, and Jeff Trask were all having coffee. What were the three of them talking about? Frank wondered. Did it have anything to do with the attack the police had interrupted?

The Hardys said a quick goodbye to Mike Clark in front of the student center. As soon as he walked away, Frank told Joe about having seen Jeff with Stan and Charlene.

"I'd give anything to know what they're talking about," he said. Through the front windows of the student center, Frank could see that Jeff and Stan had stood up and seemed to be saying goodbye to Charlene. "Here they come," he announced to his brother.

Frank dragged Joe off to the side, as Stan and Jeff emerged and said goodbye. Jeff headed off in the direction of the medical labs, and Stan strode toward University Avenue.

"Which one?" Joe asked.

"Stan," Frank decided in an instant. "We know Jeff is probably going to work. We also know he's been around for every attack on the medical labs, but we haven't linked him to the group yet—except for his being friendly with Stan. Right now, I'm more interested in Stan, since we don't know much about him."

"Let's do it," Joe said, giving his brother a low-five.

By now, Stan was far enough ahead for Frank and Joe to follow at a safe distance. When Stan reached the gate at University, Frank and Joe increased their pace enough to keep him in sight. Stan walked to the trolley stop, where he waited with a group. When the cable car came into sight, Frank and Joe edged closer to the group, then hopped on board at the back of the car.

"If he spots us, what's our cover? Where are we headed?" Joe asked his brother.

Frank looked overhead and saw a map of the cable car route. At Jackson and Mason, the route converged with another one. "The Cable Car Museum," he said, pointing to the dead end. "Right next to Chinatown, which is where we plan to have lunch. Just doing a little sightseeing, right, Joe?"

"Right," Joe confirmed.

As the cable car climbed Hyde Street and turned onto Jackson, the Hardys kept their eyes on the back of Stan's head. Sunday morning riders boarded the cable car, and others got off, but Stan didn't budge. Then, as they were approaching the Cable Car Museum, Stan stood up.

"Looks like he's got the same idea we do," said Frank. "Come on."

Frank and Joe darted off the back of the cable car just as Stan was disembarking at the front. For a moment Frank was worried that they might have lost him in the crowd around the museum, but he spotted Stan just as he was heading down Mason, toward Chinatown.

Across the street from them was a small park, and the Hardys watched as Stan went inside. "We need a plan," Frank said. "If we follow him, we won't have much cover."

The park was surrounded by bushes and trees, but the interior was wide open and didn't offer much to hide behind.

"Let's wait to see what he does," Joe said. "If he sits down, maybe we can sneak up on him through the bushes."

Stan took a seat on a bench not far from the entrance. Frank figured that he and Joe could circle around the perimeter of the park, then sneak through the bushes and come out just behind the bench where Stan was sitting.

"Come on," he urged his brother.

Just as Frank and Joe were about to cruise the outside of the park, two men headed into it. The taller one had a mustache, and the shorter, burlier guy was wearing an orange and black baseball jacket. When the Hardys crept through the bushes to the spot where Stan was sitting, Frank was able to see that the two men were sitting with Stan.

"Can you make out what they're saying?" Joe asked, kneeling beside Frank.

"I can't," said Frank. "They're speaking in a foreign language."

Frank tried to edge closer to where Stan was sitting, but the bushes thinned out too much, and he risked being seen. The two men continued talking to Stan. Several times, Frank thought he heard the word *Soong*.

"You're not going to believe me," Frank told his brother. "But I think they're talking about Soong An."

"Right," Joe said, rolling his eyes. "And I'm the Prince of Persia. Get your mind off that girl," Joe hissed.

"Shh," Frank warned his brother. He thought he saw one of the men turn to look behind him into the bushes. All at once Stan spoke to the men in English.

"You must succeed," Stan said emphatically. "Soong An must be kidnapped—or else."

Chapter

Sixteen

"**D**ID I JUST HEAR what I thought I heard?" Joe Hardy whispered to his brother. "Stan is the one who's been trying to kidnap Soong?"

"That sure is what it sounds like," Frank said quietly as he backed away. "We've got to get out of here."

Joe peered through the bushes and saw the taller of Stan's friends. He had turned around and was looking right at them through the bushes. The Hardys weren't more than five feet from the bench and Stan.

"Let's go," Joe said, backing out of the hedge.

Just as the Hardys were taking off, Joe heard one of the men call out to Stan. Over his shoulder, Joe saw the man with the mustache pointing right at them.

Frank raced toward the closest busy intersection. Joe stumbled through the bushes after his brother, taking time for one last glance at Stan and his two buddies. The three men were climbing over the bench and into the bushes, ready to give chase.

"Hurry," Frank called back to his brother.

The street was busy with traffic and pedestrians, but Stan and his cohorts weren't having any trouble gaining on the Hardys.

A cable car was clanging along trying to make the green light ahead of it. Joe didn't see a stop nearby, but he thought that they could climb aboard anyway.

"Follow me," he called out to Frank. Joe raced to catch up with the cable car. Several pedestrians stumbled out of the way as Joe cried out, "Excuse me!" The cable car picked up speed as it cruised down the hill, but Joe was determined not to let this chance to escape pass by. He rushed for the car, then lunged at the back handrail. For an excruciating second, Joe's arm felt as if it were being torn from his shoulder, but he held on.

Passengers in the cable car stared at him. Joe held fast, then hoisted himself aboard. Next to him, a frantic Frank Hardy had just caught up with the cable car and was following Joe's move. Joe reached out and pulled Frank aboard.

"Not a moment too soon," Joe said, pointing out the back. Standing in the street, frustration and defeat registering on their faces, were Stan and his two cohorts, obviously looking for a way to follow Frank and Joe. The cable car clanged merrily along, and within five minutes the Hardys had put several blocks distance between themselves and Stan.

"Well, there goes our cover," Joe announced, falling into a nearby seat. By now, the passengers had stopped staring and gone back to their books and newspapers. "Stan knows we were spying on him, and that means he has probably figured out that we're not some innocent undergraduates interested in healing the bay."

"Right," Frank said. He sank into the seat next to Joe and tried to catch his breath. "But what matters more is what *we* know about him."

"I agree," Joe said. "So what's the plan?"

"We've got to head over to the concert hall and warn Nancy," Frank said. "Soong told me that she is scheduled to play this afternoon but that she'll be watching the morning performances. Her uncle is coming in around eleven. If Stan hopes to succeed before Tim An arrives from Philonesia, he'll have to strike soon. He's running out of time."

"I bet we just witnessed their last planning session," Joe said, and felt that familiar rush of adrenaline he always got when a mystery started to heat up. "Let's just hope we get there in time."

* * *

Nancy and George had just arrived at Hammond Hall with Soong An. After her blowup the night before, Soong had stopped speaking to both Nancy and George. Since she wasn't performing until the afternoon, Soong sat on the aisle beside Erik, her violin safely cradled on her lap. She ignored Nancy and George.

"Don't worry, Nan," George said, trying to reassure her friend as they sat down a few seats away. "What matters most is that we protect Soong until her uncle gets here." George checked her watch. "Tim An should be arriving by eleven."

"Only one hour more," Nancy said with a sigh. She watched Soong chatting easily with Erik and shook her head. "I know our job was to protect Soong, but I wanted to discover who was making those calls and who the kidnappers were. I never thought I couldn't crack a case, George—this one may be my first."

"Don't give up yet," George urged. "I can look out for Soong—you question Erik. And April," George added, peeking over Nancy's shoulder.

Nancy turned to see that Soong's chaperon had arrived and was heading down the aisle to greet her charge. By now, the orchestra was slowly filing onto the stage, and the hall was filling with audience members.

Nancy checked her watch. In less than an hour, Soong would become President An's responsibility. That afternoon after the concert, President An would be holding a party for Soong at the Philonesian consulate. Tomorrow, he would try to convince her to return with him to Philonesia.

George was right, Nancy thought—she couldn't let her last chance at solving the mystery just disappear.

Nancy watched April as she sat down beside Erik. Her prime suspects were all in one place. Now it was up to Nancy to put together the questions, and the theories that would force some answers from Erik and April.

"Come with me and keep an eye on Soong, would you, George?" Nancy asked her friend as she stood up from her seat. "I want to speak with Erik and April."

"Way to go," said George. "I thought I recognized that spark in your eyes."

April smiled at Nancy brightly when she sat down next to her. "How are you?" she asked warmly. "Are you enjoying your stay in San Francisco? I hope Soong An hasn't been giving you too much trouble."

"No," Nancy said slowly. "But her kidnappers have." Nancy paused as she watched April's face for any sign of emotion. "Why is it that every time Soong lets you know where she's going to be, April, that's the exact time someone tries to snatch her?"

The woman didn't drop her elegant demeanor

for an instant. Instead, she raised a hand to pat her perfectly curled hair. "I don't know, Nancy," she said. "Maybe you can tell me."

"I'm wondering if maybe you're tipping them off," Nancy put in bluntly.

Soong, who was sitting on the other side of Erik, must have overheard Nancy, for she stopped talking to Erik and addressed Nancy. "I've told you that I trust April," Soong said angrily. "Why won't you believe me?"

"Who is the young man I've seen you with?" Nancy pressed. "He was here at the concert hall two days ago, and I think he was spying on us at Fisherman's Wharf."

April raised an eyebrow. "I don't know any spies," she said, her voice cold. "That man you saw with me the other day is, as I told you then, a relative." Then the woman checked her watch and stood up. "Now if you'll excuse me."

April edged her way past Nancy and strode up the aisle and out of the hall. Soong stiffened in her seat and went back to talking to Erik. Nancy felt her face burn at April's emphatic denials, but she decided there was no point in holding back, not now. She slid into the seat April had vacated and addressed Erik.

"I've had Soong's crank calls traced," she told him. "Guess whose phone they were made from?"

"I have no idea," Erik said. He gave both her and Soong a shrug. "Whose?"

"Yours," Nancy stated flatly.

Erik seemed stunned. "You're kidding."

"I wish I were," Nancy said.

Soong's sullen expression only intensified. "Thanks, Nancy, for accusing my best friend of having it in for me," she said.

"I simply want to know if Erik has any idea how those calls were made from his room," Nancy said.

"And who might have made them," George put in. She had sat down in the row behind them and followed every word. "We know it was a woman. We're not saying it was you, Erik."

Erik became quiet and thoughtful for a moment. Then he said, "Li has a key to my room. Could she have been the one to make the calls?"

"It's possible," Nancy said. Privately, she still felt that Erik had the best motive for harassing Soong. Li could even be his accomplice. Right now, Erik might be trying to put all the blame on Li. Then again, Nancy still couldn't prove that Erik would go so far as to threaten Soong just to help his own chances in the competition. There was Soong's ruined bow to consider—but then hadn't Erik lent Soong his own bow?

Nancy was trying to make sense of all of this, when April reappeared. "I have a surprise for you," she said to Soong. "Come out to the lobby."

Soong was up and out of her seat, with her violin case in hand, when Nancy spotted Frank and Joe Hardy racing into the rehearsal hall. "Nancy," Joe cried. "We've got to talk to you. It's urgent."

Behind them, Nancy spotted a dignified, middle-aged man. His thick head of hair was shot through with gray, and he walked with a serene, composed manner. Following were two men in dark suits and sunglasses who must have been undercover security guards.

"Soong," the man said.

"Uncle Tim," cried Soong An, racing up the aisle to greet him.

While Soong and Tim An were reunited, the Hardys caught up with Nancy. "What's going on?" Nancy asked them.

"We got a huge break—" Joe began.

"In your case," Frank finished for him.

"Soong's life is in danger," Joe said. "At this very minute."

Nancy tried to keep her eyes on Soong. At the same time she desperately wanted to question Frank and Joe. Since a performance was about to begin, Soong and her uncle decided to take their reunion outside into the lobby. Nancy, Frank, Joe, and George followed with April.

Standing in the lobby was the man Nancy recognized from Fisherman's Wharf—the one April claimed was her relative.

By now, Nancy's detective instincts were on major alert. Frank and Joe had said Soong's life was in immediate danger. Was this the man she should be worried about?

Suddenly the outside doors burst open, and two masked men entered the lobby.

"Soong," Nancy cried. "President An—those men are Soong's kidnappers."

Everything happened at once. Frank, Joe, and one of Tim An's guards raced toward the two masked men and Nancy pulled Soong toward her and George. People standing in the lobby hurried for cover, but President An stood stock-still, staring at the young man from Fisherman's Wharf.

"You!" he cried. "I told you I never wanted to see you around my niece again. What are you doing here?"

"Jeffrey," Soong called out. Nancy nearly fell over in surprise as Soong rushed into the young man's arms.

"That's Jeff Trask!" Frank Hardy cried, momentarily turning. "What's going on here?"

President An moved toward the young Philonesian man, who released Soong from his embrace. At the same time Nancy realized that in the commotion, the kidnappers were getting away.

"Let's go!" Nancy said to George. The two masked men had disappeared through the front entrance, followed by Joe, Frank, and one of Tim An's guards. "We can't let them get away."

"Oh, no, you don't," Tim An was saying, and Nancy stopped momentarily. Mr. An wasn't talking to her. "You're not getting away this time, Jeffrey Tran!" Tim An shouted.

President An and his other bodyguard tried to block the front entrance. But a group of people were entering the building, and in the confusion, Jeffrey managed to push his way past Tim An—and out the door.

Nancy raced out the door, too, following both Jeffrey and the two masked men. By now, Soong's kidnappers had escaped in a waiting car. Joe and Frank were standing on the walkway, watching as the car sped away. Jeffrey, meanwhile, was in the middle of University Avenue, hailing a cab.

"Stop him," Mr. An warned. "Stop that man."

"Piece of cake," Joe Hardy cried, when he realized President An meant Jeffrey.

Nancy, Frank, and one of the bodyguards were right behind him. Suddenly a figure dashed ahead of her and toward Jeffrey, who had by now gotten a taxi to stop for him and climbed in.

Soong An! She rushed for the cab and jumped in—still holding her violin case. Nancy watched, stunned and amazed, as Soong slammed the cab door. A moment later the taxi sped off with the screech of peeling rubber.

Soong An was gone.

Chapter

Seventeen

As Nancy watched the cab grow smaller, she couldn't believe her eyes. After everything that had happened, Nancy had lost Soong in full sight of her uncle. Soong hadn't even been kidnapped —she'd gone off of her own free will.

Dejected and embarrassed, Nancy rejoined the others on the steps of the concert hall. There, everyone in the group was talking all at once about what had happened.

"That boy will pay for this," an angry Tim An said. "I've warned him before to stay away from my niece."

"He wanted to make up with you, Tim," April said, her tone pleading. "That is why he was here. He had no intention of stealing Soong away from you. I urged him to come."

"You did!" Tim An sputtered angrily. "You know how I feel about him and his brother."

"You're wrong, Tim An," April said emphatically. "Jeffrey and Soong are in love. You were wrong to keep them apart, and you know it."

"I know only about the safety of my niece," Tim An said. "To protect it, I have insisted she stay away from Jeffrey Tran. His brother is still my most dangerous enemy. No matter what you say about Jeffrey—"

"Who no longer supports Rupert, as you know," April put in.

Nancy wanted to scream a gigantic "time out," but instead tried, as politely as possible, to get a better sense of what had just happened.

"Jeffrey is your other nephew?" she asked April. When April nodded, Nancy went on. "And he's also the person Soong was in love with—"

"*Is* in love with," April corrected. "Despite what her uncle wishes."

At this bit of information, Nancy couldn't tell who flinched more—Erik or Frank. "But Jeffrey is not the person who's been trying to kidnap her, is that what you're saying?" she asked April.

"Mr. An had forbidden Jeffrey and Soong to see each other anymore, when they were in Philonesia. Jeffrey has honored that wish, but from time to time I have given him some details about where she goes and who she is with."

"How long has this been going on?" Tim An demanded.

"Jeffrey arrived about two months ago and took the name Jeff Trask, but he had no idea when he got here that Soong was also here." April let out a long sigh. "I was the one who told him, and after that I promised to keep him informed about Soong and how she was doing. When I heard you were coming to take Soong back, I made Jeffrey promise that he would try to make amends with you, Tim An. But obviously you scared him off just now."

Suddenly Tim An looked pale and tired. Nancy thought the trip must have taken a lot out of him. Not to mention Soong's having run off with Jeffrey.

"I'm so sorry," Nancy said, apologizing to Tim An. "I should have been more careful."

"I don't get it," George chimed in. "If Jeffrey's not the kidnapper, then who is?"

"Finally!" Joe Hardy practically shouted. "Someone asks the right question."

The group turned to Joe. By now, Nancy could hear the strains of the orchestra coming from inside the concert hall. To passing traffic, they must have seemed like a strange sight: Tim An with his bodyguards, Nancy, George, Erik, Frank, and April—all standing and staring at Joe Hardy.

"Because we have the answer," Joe said proudly.

Nancy listened as Frank and Joe quickly related how they'd overheard Stan talking to the two men who they believed were Soong's kidnappers. One of Tim An's bodyguards said he thought he had recognized one of the men. Now he was sure of it.

"You actually heard Stan saying they had to get Soong, or else?" Nancy said. "I can't believe it. Who is this guy, and why would he be after Soong?" Before Frank or Joe could answer, Nancy put another question to them. "Why were you following him anyway?"

"Stan's a suspect in our case," Frank explained.

When Tim An and April stared at the Hardys and Nancy with quizzical expressions, Nancy explained that Frank and Joe were also detectives. Finally Nancy got to hear more about what Frank and Joe had been working on. They explained about how they'd infiltrated Ethics Now and that they'd actually been arrested that morning. Frank shared with them his suspicions that Charlene might have been the one to tip off the police.

"Wait a second," Nancy said. "Are you talking about Stan Jones, Charlene's boyfriend? The Philonesian guy?"

"Must be the same one, " Joe said.

"We've also been keeping an eye on Jeff Trask because he's been in the medical labs every time an act of sabotage occurred," Frank added. "We had no idea he had changed his name, and so far we haven't definitely linked him to Ethics Now."

At this April spoke up. "Jeffrey—I prefer to call him that—would never do anything against the university. He wants only to work in peace. In fact, he changed his last name because there are many Philonesian students at SFU, and he didn't want to be associated with his brother."

Nancy was dumbfounded to know that all along Jeffrey Tran, or Jeff Trask, had been a player in both her case and the Hardys'. "If only you'd seen Jeffrey that night at Fisherman's Wharf," she said, "we'd have put a lot of this together sooner."

"Something else occurs to me," George offered. "It sounds like Charlene's been pretty important in all this."

"How do you mean?" Nancy asked.

George pointed out what was now obvious. "Charlene could have helped Stan figure out Soong's whereabouts. Remember what Soong said about her schedule being stolen. What if Stan took it one of the times he was over at the suite?"

"That means Stan could have been using Charlene all along," said Nancy. "She could have been feeding Stan information this whole time. Charlene and Stan both knew we were going for a picnic, and they knew about our going to Groove."

"I doubt Charlene's been a willing accomplice to Stan's plan," George said, defending the girl.

"I'd have to agree," Frank said. "From what

we've seen at Ethics Now meetings, Charlene cares a lot about the group."

"Listen," Frank said, tapping his foot impatiently. "What matters most right now is that we find Jeff and Soong—before Stan and his goons get to them."

"You're absolutely right," Nancy said. "I've got a few loose ends to tie up," she added, thinking of Li Bao, "but why don't we work together on this from now on?"

April exchanged a nervous glance with Tim An. "Shouldn't we involve the police at this point?"

President An pursed his lips and thought for a moment. "I don't want to create any kind of incident, especially now that I'm out of my country. I trust Nancy and her friends, and I believe they will be able to find Soong and Jeffrey. At this point the fewer people who know about what is happening, the better." President An gestured to his bodyguards. "We will go to the consulate. You can reach me there," he said to Nancy. "I will return at three when Soong is scheduled to perform. She is headstrong and stubborn, but her music means everything to her. I do not think she will give up her chance to compete in such a prestigious event."

Nancy now noticed the limousine parked on the street in front of the concert hall. Tim An strode toward it purposefully, and the driver hurried to open the back door. Tim An's bodyguards followed him into the waiting car. Moments later the limousine was pulling into traffic.

April let out a long sigh after Tim An was gone. "I hope we are doing the right thing. I am so worried about Soong An."

For the first time Nancy was embarrassed to accuse April of having had something to do with Soong's kidnapping. If they were right about Charlene and Stan, then April hadn't been tipping off the kidnappers to Soong's whereabouts. Nancy apologized to the woman, who smiled in understanding.

"You were doing your job," April said to Nancy. "I'm sorry I couldn't explain to you about Jeffrey and Soong." April said her goodbyes and headed to the street to hail a cab.

"We need a plan," Nancy said to Frank, Joe, and George. "George and I should go back to the dorm to see if Li—"

"She's not a suspect, is she?" Joe Hardy asked, surprised.

"We think Li may have used Erik's phone to make harassing calls to Soong," George put in.

"We don't know that for sure," Erik insisted. "I simply said she had a key." He sighed and ran a hand through his dark, wavy hair. "What's going on around here?" he wondered out loud. "How did everything get so crazy?"

Nancy could tell Erik was worried about

Soong. "Let's all head back to campus," she said. "You look like you could use a break," she told Erik.

"I need some lunch," Erik said weakly. "If my stomach's empty, the whole world looks bad."

Nancy and the Hardys decided that while Nancy and George went to question Li, Frank and Joe would try to locate Jeff and Soong. "We'll get his address from Dean Harper or from his boss at the labs. Don't worry," Frank assured Nancy. "We'll find them."

"Let's keep in contact," said Nancy. "Call and leave a message on Soong's answering machine if you get any leads. Then we can all meet back here at three. That's when Soong's supposed to perform. I agree with her uncle—I doubt that she'd give up her shot at winning this competition."

"I know you're right," Erik put in, his face brightening a bit at Nancy's suggestion.

"Let's just hope Stan doesn't find Jeffrey and Soong before then," George added.

Nancy, George, and Erik wished Frank and Joe luck and said goodbye. Then the trio headed over to campus. While Erik went on ahead to the dining hall to grab some lunch, Nancy and George went to the dorm, in the hopes of finding Li there. She wasn't, but as soon as Nancy and George entered the suite, the phone rang. Nancy went to pick up the receiver and heard the familiar voice of Soong's harasser.

"Tell Soong An her chances of living grow dimmer every day," the woman said and hung up.

Nancy replaced the receiver. Quickly she dialed *69. The same woman answered the phone and said in a confused voice, "Hello?"

Nancy hung up and hustled George out of the suite. "Come on," she urged. "We've got to get to Erik's room—and fast."

On the first floor, Nancy looked down the corridor in dismay. She had no idea where Erik's room was. She was about to turn and head back to Soong's suite, when Li Bao emerged from a room at the end of the hall. At first, Li seemed surprised to see Nancy and George, but she regained her composure fairly quickly.

"Nancy! George!" she said as she pulled the door shut behind her. "What are you doing here?"

"I was about to ask you the same question," Nancy said. "Isn't that Erik Kolker's room?" she asked, bluffing.

Li looked behind her, then turned back to Nancy and George. "I was just leaving him a note. I still have a key, so I let myself in."

"You didn't make a phone call by any chance, did you?" George asked.

For a moment Li appeared startled. Then she smiled, a bit too brightly, Nancy thought, and said, "No, why?"

"Because someone's been using Erik's phone to make harassing calls to Soong An," said Nancy. "We think it's you."

"Me?" Li placed her hand to her chest, in a gesture of innocence. "I can't believe what I'm hearing. Why would I do a thing like that?"

"To scare Soong into going home," Nancy replied.

Li obviously wanted to force Soong to go home so that she could have Erik all to herself. It also occurred to Nancy that Li had probably ruined Soong's bow, in a desperate move to force Soong out of the competition and help Erik win. All the facts were coming together, and Nancy confronted Li with her theory.

"I am insulted," the girl stated flatly. "Erik has a great chance of winning without my help. And as for Soong, we all know she is in very real danger of being kidnapped. Why would I want to scare her any more than she is already?"

"From the day we got here," George pointed out, "you've told Soong she should go home. How do we know you haven't done something more to make sure she would?"

Before Li could answer, Nancy abruptly changed the subject. "Erik told me he's expecting an important phone call. Did the phone happen to ring while you were in his room?"

Li seemed relieved to find herself off the hook. She smiled and said, "Actually, it did. I answered it, but whoever called just hung up."

Bingo. Nancy and George exchanged a look of triumph.

"Li, we know you're the person who's been making the calls," Nancy said firmly. "That call you answered was from me—I was tracing the one you'd just made to Soong."

Li drew in a sharp breath, then let it out slowly. From her expression, Nancy could see that Li knew she'd been caught.

"Why don't you tell us about it?" Nancy asked gently. "And start at the beginning."

Frank and Joe Hardy were walking along a short, quiet block. What had started as a gorgeous, sunny day had turned into a cloudy, overcast one. Joe shivered and pulled up his jacket collar as he and Frank walked up the block. The university operator had been able to give them Jeff Trask's home phone number and address. The Hardys had tried to reach Jeff by phone, but no one answered. They decided, after grabbing a quick lunch, to head over to Jeff's place and stake it out, hoping that Jeff would come home.

As Joe Hardy approached the building where Jeff lived, he felt both excited and apprehensive. If Jeff was home by now, was Soong with him? And would he be willing to let Soong go? Jeff probably wasn't dangerous, but there was still too much that Frank and Joe didn't know—for example, had Jeff been one of Stan's accomplices from the very beginning, despite what April had said?

The place where Jeff lived was a two-story brick building with a garage on the ground floor. Frank walked up the stairs to the front entrance and rang the bell. When no one answered, Frank looked at Joe and shrugged.

"The front door's open," he pointed out.

"So let's go inside," Joe said. He pushed open the front door, to find himself inside a dingy hallway. The paint was peeling, and the linoleum on the floor was coming up.

"Nice place," Joe said.

"His apartment must be upstairs," Frank said, gesturing. "The operator told me number four."

Joe Hardy hiked up the narrow staircase. At the top, he spotted apartment three. Next to it was a door with a four on it. "Here we go," Joe said.

He knocked on the door. There was no answer, but then Joe heard footsteps behind the door. "Who is it?" a voice demanded.

"Jeff, it's Frank and Joe Hardy," Frank said, leaning toward the door. "Why don't you let us in? We need to talk to you about Soong."

Joe then heard the sound of several men laughing. "What the—?" he began.

The door swung open to reveal Stan Jones, along with his two cohorts. The man with the mustache was laughing heartily, and the stocky one next to him had a terrifying grin on his face.

"Not who we expected, eh, boys?" Stan asked, turning to the other men. "But you kids will do. Come on in."

Joe froze. What could they do? He eyed Frank for some sign of a plan, but his brother seemed as surprised as he was. There was only one choice, and that was to get out of there—fast.

"Frank, quick," Joe urged his brother. He grabbed Frank's arm and dragged him away from the door.

Stan's men were even quicker to react. The tall one with the mustache lunged for Frank and took him out with a sharp blow to the head. Frank Hardy slumped to the floor at Joe's feet, unconscious.

Stan himself grabbed for Joe. "This one's mine," he said. "Heal the bay, huh?" he taunted. "Surfer dudes—right."

With one hand the man held Joe by the front of his jacket, and Joe got a nice close-up of Stan's nasty expression. Joe struggled in the man's grip. He lashed out with his legs, trying to kick the man's shins. The guy held Joe firm. Then the man pulled back his other arm and with his fist caught Joe square on the side of his head.

Joe moaned, and then everything went black.

Chapter

Eighteen

TWO-THIRTY FOUND NANCY fidgeting in her seat in the concert hall. The last performer before Soong had finished her concerto, and the audience was applauding enthusiastically.

Everyone except Nancy and George, that was. On one side of her George sat biting her fingernails. On the other, were two empty seats.

"Where are Joe and Frank, and where is Soong?" Nancy asked George as the applause died down.

"I wish I knew," George said, looking around. To their right and a few rows ahead she saw President An, April, and Erik. Judging by Tim An and April's expressions, they were worried about Soong, too.

Soong's performance was scheduled to begin

in less than half an hour, and it was the very last one of the Young Performers competition. The press had shown up to find out the name of the winner, which would be announced after the intermission that followed Soong's performance. The rumors had begun to spread that Soong An, the favorite and the last to perform, was AWOL.

Nancy was worried about Soong, but she was even more worried about Frank and Joe. She'd tried calling their room several times before she and George headed over to Hammond, but there had been no answer. There wasn't time to track them down at Jeff's however, once she and George ate a quick lunch and changed into clothes for the reception scheduled at the consulate after the competition.

"They'll show up," George assured her friend. "Look—" She pointed to the aisle. A chagrined Li Bao, her head hung low, was sneaking into a row of seats across from Erik, President An, and April. With Li was Charlene. Nancy knew that both girls were invited to the consulate for Soong's party, although she doubted Li would come.

"Poor Li," George said.

Nancy knew exactly what George meant. After she was confronted, a tearful Li admitted to having made the phone calls to Soong—but only after Soong had received her first threat. She saw it as an opportunity to scare Soong, and maybe even improve Erik's chances of winning. Li also admitted that she was the one to cut through Soong's bow strings and that she had left the doll on Soong's door.

"All because she's still crazy about Erik," George said, shaking her head sadly. "That's what love will do to you."

"No kidding," Nancy said. "Think about Jeffrey and Soong."

"Or Frank," George kidded. "He nearly fell in San Francisco Bay, just because of a girl."

Nancy laughed. "Thanks for that, George. I needed it." Then she grew serious. "Charlene still looks upset, too," Nancy observed.

"No wonder," George said. "You informed her that her boyfriend is a wanted kidnapper."

Nancy sighed. After she and George talked to Li, they had also managed to ask Charlene about Stan and about Soong's missing schedule. The young woman maintained that she knew nothing about Stan's involvement, and Nancy had to believe her. Charlene had been stunned and surprised, and she had seemed more than a little hurt at the thought of her own boyfriend being involved in something so dangerous. Then she informed Nancy and George that she had decided to break up with him anyway—as if she had any choice at this point—since she and Stan had gotten into a huge fight about Ethics Now and their tactics.

Still, even with these threads resolved, Nancy didn't feel happy. She tried not to think about how her stomach was twisted into knots. Not only had she blown it with Soong, she'd also possibly jeopardized the Hardys' lives.

"Where are they?" she asked herself again. If the Hardys didn't show up soon, she knew that something was wrong, very wrong.

A wave of applause made its way through the hall, distracting Nancy. The audience craned forward, and Nancy saw the reason for the sudden commotion.

A very beautiful, and very serene, Soong An stood onstage before the orchestra. She was dressed in a full-length maroon velvet dress, and her hair was in a sophisticated French knot. She held her violin with professional confidence, and when a voice called out her name as the final contestant, Soong took a commanding bow.

Nancy saw April Jost impulsively embrace Tim An. Erik smiled from ear to ear. Even Nancy found herself beaming with relief and surprise. The orchestra began to play, and Soong raised her instrument to her chin and closed her eyes, as if in a trance.

Soon, Nancy was lost in the same trance. From the first somber tones, through the dancing melodies and the exciting pizzicato sections, Soong was a master of her instrument, and the piece. Nancy found herself lost in a musical story. Soong put her heart into the final section of the piece, a driving, intense, extremely difficult portion.

When the last notes of the orchestra faded, there was a moment of silence, and then the entire audience was on its feet, giving Soong a standing ovation.

"Wow," George said.

"Double wow," Nancy said as she joined the audience in the standing ovation. "That was incredible."

Soong took a bow, her face glowing with pride. Then she rushed from the stage. A few moments later she reappeared, from a door at the side of the hall, her violin case in hand. She ran down the aisle and into her uncle's arms. Tim An gave her a huge kiss and a proud embrace, and the audience burst into another round of applause.

"Now comes the even harder part," George said. "Intermission, and then the final word."

"I think I know who won," Nancy said, moving toward Soong. She watched as Soong embraced April and then Erik. Even Li stepped across the aisle to give Soong a congratulatory hug.

"Let's wait until they announce who won," said Soong, "before you all assume I deserve congratulations."

Nancy caught Soong's eye, and the smile the girl gave her assured Nancy that all was forgiven. Tim An was trying to get his niece to explain what had happened and to tell them where Jeffrey was, but Soong wouldn't budge.

"I promised," she said. "All I am allowed to

say is that Jeffrey wants to make peace with you, Uncle Tim. He is afraid you will not want that. He will come to my party and try to reason with you."

"I will not receive him," Tim An stated firmly.

"Uncle Tim—" Soong began.

"Enough," said the man. "This trouble must not spoil your day."

Soong slipped out of her uncle's embrace, a worried expression on her face.

The audience left the hall for a brief intermission. The whole time, Nancy scanned the crowd and the entrance, watching for Frank and Joe, but they were nowhere in sight. When a bell announced that the audience should return to their seats, Nancy reluctantly returned to the hall.

Once the audience had sat back down, the contest officials stepped onto the stage. A stately woman in a full-length black dress came to the microphone. "It is the unanimous opinion of the judges that the winner of this year's Young Performers Award is Soong An. Soong, will you come to the stage to receive your prize?"

The room burst into appreciative applause. Soong An leapt up and embraced April and Erik yet again. Then she handed her violin case to April and ran to the stage to accept her award. In the front row photographers' strobes went off and reporters shouted out their questions to her.

"She deserved it," said Nancy, watching a

beaming Soong An accept the medal being placed around her neck. "She was definitely the best."

"No contest," George agreed.

For the next half an hour Soong had her picture taken and answered reporters' questions. Nancy went into the lobby to call Frank and Joe in their dorm room yet again, but there still was no answer. Then she went outside and scanned the street. She walked over to the main campus and looked around as well. Then she returned to the hall and tried the Hardys' dorm room again. By that time, Soong was finished with her first round of interviews, and the group was ready to head over to the consulate for her party.

"Good thing I won," Soong said, smiling widely. "Or else we wouldn't want to celebrate, right, Uncle Tim?"

"I can think of another reason to celebrate," Tim An said slowly. He was watching Soong as she accepted the congratulations of the audience members who had lingered after the competition.

"Why?" Soong asked. "You will let me see Jeffrey?"

Tim An laughed slightly. "You just don't give up, do you? No. I've been thinking, actually, that if we could be sure of your safety, I might let you stay here in the United States."

"Yeaaah!" Soong threw her arms around her uncle in an ecstatic hug. "I can't believe it. Why did you change your mind?"

"I said *if,*" Tim An warned. "You will still need bodyguards, and they must be of my choosing. But I have been thinking that you have a tremendous career ahead of you, and who am I to stand in your way?"

"You're right, Uncle Tim, now we do have something to celebrate. Come on, I feel like dancing."

Nancy and George followed the group out of the concert hall.

"What should we do about Frank and Joe?" Nancy asked George.

"Hope they're all right?" George said with a wince. "I don't know what else we can do."

Nancy knew her friend was right. Around her, everyone was eager to start celebrating. Nancy wished she could be as lighthearted as Soong An, but with Frank and Joe missing, and Stan Jones still at large, her thoughts were far more serious.

At the Philonesian consulate, there was a buffet of delicious appetizers in the parlor, and a jazz band in the main lobby. A crowd of Tim An's friends and supporters milled throughout the downstairs rooms. Nancy spotted Wendy Kim talking to what looked like a group of Philonesian businessmen. Jeff still hadn't shown up, but both Soong and April were looking for him. Erik was dancing with Li, and Charlene and Soong were talking.

While Erik and Li danced, Nancy and George

watched from an upstairs balcony. The balcony ran around the entire room. On one side there was a staircase leading down to the lobby. On the other were tall French doors that led to another balcony outdoors. From where they stood, Nancy and George could see the entire party in the lobby just below them.

"Soong seems very happy," George said.

"She does," Nancy agreed. "I just wish I felt as carefree."

"Maybe we should call the police," George suggested. "Or get in touch with Dean Harper?"

"You're right," said Nancy. "But we can't call the police without telling Tim An. Somehow we've got to convince him that it's definitely time to get the police involved. Before we do that, though, I'll get Jeff's number and try to reach him."

Nancy was about to head back downstairs, when she noticed that one of the tall doors leading from the balcony to the outdoors was slowly opening. Suddenly a man appeared.

It was Stan Jones!

Not a second later, Stan was flanked by his two henchmen.

"George," Nancy cried. "Look!"

"It's Jones," said George. "We've got to stop him."

The balcony ran around the interior of the room, but the French doors Jones had stepped through were on the far side from where Nancy and George were standing. She would either have to race around the balcony to that side to catch Jones, or she would have to stop him at the stairway.

Gasping, Nancy saw that there wasn't time to do either. Rather than running around to the stairs, Jones leapt from the balcony down to the carpeted lobby below. There, Nancy saw Soong jump with fright. Erik and Tim An tried to protect her, but it was too late.

Stan Jones grabbed Soong with one arm and pressed a gun into her side with the other. "Nobody move," he warned. "Or the girl dies."

Chapter

Nineteen

Nancy saw only one option. If Stan could jump from the balcony, so could she. She climbed over the railing, and, without a second thought, jumped.

Nancy made a bone-jarring landing and saw that behind her George had also taken the leap.

The moves startled Stan, who whirled around and aimed his gun in their direction. In the meantime Stan's henchmen had run down the stairs. Erik used the opportunity to grab one of Stan's henchmen, but the guy simply knocked Erik out cold.

By now Tim An had called his guards. The room filled with half a dozen armed men. Even Stan could tell he was outnumbered. For a moment Nancy thought the man would release Soong, but she was wrong.

"I mean it, An," said Jones. "In the name of my friend and fellow freedom-fighter Rupert Tran, I will kill your niece if any of you take a step closer."

Stan Jones pulled Soong An tighter. The young woman squirmed. Her eyes widened with fright, but she didn't make a sound.

The room grew hushed. The president stared down his enemy. "Lower your weapons," he told his guards. "I will make you pay for this, Stan Junpei."

Jones retreated from the room, holding Soong An before him as a shield. His cohorts followed. The second they left Nancy rushed after them.

Around them, Tim An's guards looked to him for instructions, but Nancy didn't stop to wait—and neither did George.

"I'm right behind you, Nan," she said. "This is the part I like—the athletic part."

In the circular driveway outside the embassy, Nancy was in for another shock. Jeffrey Tran had just pulled up and had faced off with Stan.

"What are you doing with Soong?" Jeffrey demanded.

"You don't get it, do you?" Stan replied, holding the gun to Soong's side. By now, his henchmen had pulled their car up to the entrance to the consulate. They squealed to a stop in front of Stan, and the back door flew open.

"Let's go," the shorter one shouted to Stan.

Tim An came running from the consulate, along with his guards and April.

"See you back home in Philonesia," Stan said to Jeffrey and the others. "We will be in touch, Tim An. Don't let any of your men follow us, if you know what's good for Soong An. Once we see that you've followed our instructions, we will let you know about our demands. Rest assured— you won't see your niece alive again until Rupert Tran is in charge of our country. Long live the rebel forces."

With that, Stan dragged Soong to the backseat of the waiting car. He pushed her inside, got in, and slammed the door shut behind him. In a burst of speed the driver pulled away from the consulate.

"They're getting away!" George cried in frustration.

"Not if we can help it," Nancy said. She searched the consulate driveway. There were three official-looking cars parked there, along with those belonging to Tim An's guests. "Can we use one of these cars?"

"That's not necessary," Jeffrey said. He pointed to his beat-up compact car.

Nancy hopped into the front seat, while George squeezed into the back. In the dusky light, Tim An's expression was anguished. "Find my niece," he said. "Do whatever you can to find her and save her. But do not risk her life."

Jeffrey peeled out of the consulate driveway. Nancy looked behind her to see that Tim An's guards were also piling into nearby cars.

"This isn't good," said Nancy. "If Stan sees all these people following him, he may harm Soong."

"Don't forget we might need the backup," George reminded her.

"You're right," Nancy agreed reluctantly, "but I'm just worried about what Stan might do."

"Which you should," Jeffrey confirmed. "I thought I knew him well, but I would never have predicted this from him."

Stan's car came into sight at the bottom of a hill. "There they are," Nancy said. "Try to stay close enough to follow him, but not so close that he realizes we're after him."

"Okay," Jeff said. He sped through one yellow light, then passed a slow-moving car in the right lane.

Stan's car turned right at the bottom of the hill, heading toward the bay. Jeffrey made it to the next light just as it was changing from yellow to red. Nancy turned and saw that Tim An's men from the consulate had gotten caught at a red light. There was too much cross-traffic for them to go through it, and Nancy saw one of them banging his hands on the steering wheel in frustration.

Looking ahead again, Nancy saw that Stan was taking a series of turns—first a left toward

195

Fisherman's Wharf, then a right that led them closer to the bay, and downtown. He drove through downtown and under the freeway that led to the Bay Bridge. Now they were in a more desolate area of the city, where there were warehouses and a lot of truck traffic.

"Hold on," Jeff warned as he followed at a clip. "I'm not going to lose him now."

The car bumped over a series of potholes and climbed another hill, away from the bay. They passed a cable car turnaround, and a marina on their left. Finally Stan took another series of turns, and Nancy found that they were heading back to the wharf. Only this time, there were no pedestrians on the streets—only desolate, commercial buildings.

"Slow down," Nancy warned Jeffrey. "We don't have much cover now, and we don't want them to see us."

Stan's car was coming to a stop in front of a brick warehouse building. From the broken windows and boarded-up entrance, Nancy was pretty sure the place was empty—a good spot for Stan to hide Soong until he could get her out of the country.

Rather than pull up on the street and risk being seen, Jeffrey coolly backed his car into a nearby alley. From there they had a clear view of the warehouse. Stan's men removed the boards from the door and entered the building.

"They're taking her inside," Jeffrey said, his face contorted in anger. "I'd like to storm them right now and beat the daylights out of Stan."

"We need to stay levelheaded," Nancy reminded him.

"And we need a plan," George put in.

"Let's wait for them to get inside," said Nancy. "Then we can sneak in after them, check out the layout of the place, and see if there isn't some way to surprise them."

They waited a good five minutes. From the wharf came the sound of foghorns. Now that the sun had completely set, Nancy realized that the fog was moving in quickly. She could barely make out the buildings farther down the street.

"Okay," she said. "Let's go. Be quiet and be careful. Most important, stick together."

Nancy led the way across the street. The door to the warehouse was open, and Nancy, George, and Jeffrey entered quietly. Once they were inside, Nancy shuddered—from the damp, the dark, and the sight of the place. A staircase ahead of them was falling apart. Several steps were missing, and Nancy doubted it would hold their weight. In the distance, to their left, Nancy heard the sound of voices.

She edged slowly down a short hallway that led to another that ran the length of the building. On the right were a series of doors. On the left were several large rooms separated by shoulder-high walls. Nancy thought that there had probably once been glass partitions going all the way to the ceiling.

Nancy could hear voices at the end of the hallway, and she could see a dim light.

"Keep down," she warned Jeff and George. All three of them crept into the first room, keeping well below the level of the walls. Nancy quietly moved to the wall separating the first room from the second. Since it was so dark, Nancy knew that if she was quiet and moved slowly she wouldn't be spotted. Carefully she stood up, just long enough to look over the wall. She saw Soong sitting alone on a chair in the last room, her hands tied behind her and her feet bound to the legs of the chair. There was a battery-operated lamp on a table near her.

"I see her," Nancy said, backing away a bit.

"Do you see Stan or his men?" George asked, keeping down.

"No," Nancy whispered. "My guess is that they're in the last room on the right—at least that's where it sounds like their voices are coming from. Follow me."

Nancy knelt and edged along the wall of the first room and into the hallway. When she got to the doorway into the second room, she turned and gestured for George and Jeff to follow.

In the gloom, she could barely make out their dark forms as they crawled toward her. Now they were just on the other side of the wall from Soong.

"Keep down," Nancy whispered, "I'm going to climb over the wall to get Soong. If I get caught, you two get out of here as fast as you can and call the police." Nancy no longer cared whether or not Tim An wanted the police involved. This was a life-and-death situation now.

George and Jeff nodded in understanding.

"Be careful, Nan," George whispered.

"I will," Nancy said. She crept quietly along the wall, wanting to get as far from the hallway as possible, before she climbed over.

From a room across the way came Stan's voice, louder and more insistent. Good, Nancy thought. Let him be too busy arguing to worry about what's going on out here.

Slowly Nancy stood up and peeked over the dividing wall. She was relieved to see that Soong was still alone.

Just then Soong looked up, and her eyes widened in surprise. Nancy motioned for her to be silent. Then she pulled herself up and over the dividing wall and dropped down on Soong's side. Quickly she ran over to Soong and began untying her hands. She had almost freed Soong's hands when Nancy realized something was wrong. She didn't hear Stan's voice any longer. What had happened?

Nancy looked through the doorway—and had

her answer. George and Jeffrey were being pushed into the room by Stan's two cohorts. Stan had his gun trained on George's and Jeffrey's backs.

"You thought you'd outsmart me?" Stan demanded of the trio. "Guess again!"

"Bo!" Stan called out to the heavyset man guarding George and Jeffrey. "Grab this pest"—he gestured to Nancy with his gun—"and let her have a last look at her friends before we do away with them all."

Chapter
Twenty

FRANK HARDY regained consciousness in a darkened room that smelled of old paint and cigarettes. His head was pounding and his stomach felt as if it had been walked on.

Next to him, Frank saw his brother, Joe, still out cold. Frank moved to wake him up, only to discover that his own hands were tied behind his back and his feet were bound to the same rope.

"Good luck, Hardy," Frank muttered to himself. "You've been down before, but never this bad."

In the distance Frank thought he heard voices: a man's, a woman's, and even a voice that sounded like Nancy's. "You're hearing things," he told himself. "Must have been that knock on the head you got."

Every time Frank moved, his head pounded even harder. Vaguely, he remembered getting knocked out by Stan Jones, but he had no idea how he'd gotten from the hallway of Jeff's apartment, where he'd last been, to the rat hole he was in now.

"Uhhnn," Joe Hardy murmured, his eyelids fluttering open. "Where are we?"

Frank scanned the dismal walls once more. Outside, he heard the distinctive low tones of a foghorn. "Close to the water," he told his brother. "I can't tell you much more."

"Who's that talking?" Joe wondered aloud. "It sounds like Nancy."

"You know, I thought the same thing," Frank said. "Do you really think it's her?"

Frank listened more carefully, trying not to let his hope take over too much. But the more he heard, the surer he was. He couldn't make out the words, but Nancy seemed to be trying to reason with someone. And when a man replied, Frank was almost certain he recognized Stan Jones's voice.

"Looks-like Stan's brought us all together," Frank said to Joe. "And that can't be good news for any of us."

"Wrong," Joe corrected his brother. "As soon as we get out of these ropes, it's bad news for him."

"And how are we going to do that?" Frank asked.

"There's got to be something in this place that we can use to cut through them," said Joe. "Look around."

Frank rolled over onto his side and slowly fishtailed across the floor, looking for any kind of sharp object. At one point, he felt the sleeve of his jacket catch on something. Once he maneuvered around to see what it was, Frank discovered a loose nail.

"I think I've got it," he told Joe. "Come here and help me dig this out."

Working together, and back to back, the Hardys managed to remove the loose nail from the floorboard. By now, Frank felt exhausted, and his head was still a pounding nightmare. The work had just begun.

"I'll see what I can do about cutting through your rope," he said to Joe. They were still lying back to back. Frank felt for the part of the rope that went from Joe's hands to his feet. He used the tip of the nail to pull apart the rope. Soon, he could feel that it had frayed, at least part of the way. "Try pulling it apart," Frank instructed Joe, turning around to face him.

Joe rolled over so that he was now facing Frank. He yanked his feet away from his hands. Frank watched his brother struggle. At first it seemed as if Frank would have to take another shot at cutting through the rope. But suddenly Joe's eyes gleamed victoriously, and his hands and his feet were separated.

"I think the rope's loose enough now for me to get my hands free," Joe said, squirming. "Yes!" he announced. He pulled one hand loose and then the other. "Turn back around. I'll get you."

Within a few seconds Joe had Frank's ropes untied. Frank sat up and rubbed his chafed wrists. "That feels great," he said, standing up and heading for the door. "You got your lockpick?" he asked Joe.

"I did," said Joe, checking his back pocket. "But not now."

"Why am I not surprised?" Frank asked. "Give me that nail," he said, holding his hand out to Joe. "This is an old lock. We should be able to get through it pretty easily."

Sure enough, Frank had the door unlocked with a few swift moves. He opened it slowly and saw the door led onto a narrow, dim hallway. There were shoulder-high walls dividing the length of the warehouse into rooms. Frank caught a glimpse of Stan and his men in a room at the end of the building. Vaguely, he was aware that Nancy, Soong, Jeff, and George were also there.

"Yikes," Frank said under his breath.

He ducked quickly, to keep out of sight. He signaled Joe to do the same. Once they were down, the Hardys could only see some light and hear voices.

"That's Nancy all right. George is with her, too. Soong and Jeff are there, and Stan has them all hostage." Frank slumped against the wall. "We need a plan, and it had better be good."

"What's the layout?" Joe asked.

Frank briefly explained what little he'd seen.

"Okay," said Joe. "Here's an idea. How about if we sneak down the hallway. You go into the room next to the one they're in. I'll wait outside the door. You go over the wall, and I'll rush them through the door. That way we can come at them from both directions."

"Sounds good," Frank agreed.

Carefully Frank and Joe crept down the hallway. At the second door Frank whispered, "Follow me in here first. Let's get an idea of what's going on there." He nodded in the direction of the last room.

"Okay," Joe said.

In the darkness of the second room, Frank stood up just enough to see into the room where Stan and his men held Nancy and the others prisoner. Frank saw that Nancy, George, Soong, and Jeff all had their hands tied behind their backs. Nancy and George were on the floor, while Soong and Jeff were sitting on flimsy, straightbacked chairs. Frank ducked down again. He could distinctly make out Stan and Nancy arguing, along with another man and a woman who sounded like Jeff and Soong.

"So you were responsible for the attacks on the medical labs, too," Nancy was saying. "Why?"

"I wanted to scare Jeff into returning home, to be by his brother's side where he belonged," Stan replied.

"I have repudiated my brother," Jeff insisted. "And it's because he condones tactics such as this one. I will not join him again for anything."

"Listen to you!" Stan shouted. "You are naive. You think Tim An is any better?"

"It doesn't matter," Jeff insisted. "You claimed to be my friend. You introduced yourself to me as a fellow Philonesian, and told me about all our friends in common. But the whole time you were plotting against me. Even my brother was willing to harm me and the woman I love."

"Don't argue with him," Soong said. "Don't even sink to his level."

"I should have sought you out when I first learned you were in San Francisco," Jeff said to Soong. "We could have avoided all this."

"Now is not the time to have second thoughts," Soong said. "What matters is that we are together now, and we will be together in the future. Once my uncle puts this crook behind bars, which is what he deserves."

"Enough!" Stan shouted. "I will not argue with you any longer. Bo, get the others. We'll put them all in this room and then set the place on fire. No one will care about a warehouse accident, and by then we'll be long gone with Soong."

"My uncle will not let you get away with this!" Soong shouted.

Frank turned and looked for Joe. He knew they didn't have much time. As soon as Stan's goons discovered that he and Joe weren't still tied up, they'd start looking for them.

Frank discovered Joe in the far corner, tying together several lengths of rope. "You can't go out in the hallway. They're about to look for us," Frank whispered. "What are you doing, anyway?"

Joe pointed to an oversize hook in the ceiling between the room they were in, and the room where Stan held Nancy and the others. "If we can get this rope through that hook, then I think I can swing over the wall and take them all by surprise."

"That's crazy," Frank told his brother.

"You got another idea?" Joe asked. When Frank didn't answer, Joe shrugged. "So help me out, okay?"

"Okay," Frank agreed. He froze momentarily when he heard footsteps in the hallway. In the dim light he saw two figures moving down the hallway toward the room where he and Joe had been held captive. "Now!" he whispered urgently.

Frank peered over the wall. Stan had his back to them. "Hurry," Frank said, looking over the wall again.

Stan's henchmen had reappeared and were standing in the doorway.

"They're gone!" one of the men announced.

"Hurry," Joe urged. "Come here and hoist me up."

Frank rushed over to his brother and pulled on the rope until Joe was swinging off the floor. "Ready?" he asked Joe.

"I think so," Joe said.

"Here goes!"

Frank held on to the rope with one hand, and used the other to push Joe so that he went flying. As soon as Joe swung over the dividing wall, Frank rushed right after him, taking the wall with a single gigantic leap.

"Frank!" Soong cried. "Joe!"

Nancy turned to see Frank and Joe Hardy storming the room. In the tumult, Nancy used the opportunity to lash out at Stan Jones with a karate kick. The blow toppled the man.

Joe rushed over and untied Nancy. "Joe," Nancy warned him. "Look out."

The shorter of Stan's henchmen came at Joe, fists bared. Nancy was already free, and she was able to help Joe turn on the man. Once they had him out of commission, Nancy untied George, while Joe went to help his brother.

Frank had gone after the other goon. The Hardys went at the man from both angles, but it was George who put him out finally.

"Stand back!" she cried. And then she went flying at the man, her legs lashing out in a series of lightning moves. "Yeah!"

The man slumped to the ground. George was triumphant. "That felt good. My kickboxing training is paying off, huh?"

Stan Jones was rising to his feet and was reaching for the gun he'd dropped when Nancy knocked him over.

"I don't think so," she said, kicking the gun out of the way. "It's four against one, Jones, and this time I think that means you're pretty much outnumbered. Give it up."

Jones fell back to the floor. His plot to kidnap Soong An and to get Jeff Tran home had been stopped.

Two hours later the group was taking a well-earned rest in the Philonesian consulate's outdoor garden. Chinese lanterns were strung across a brick patio, and the air smelled of jasmine and roses. Nancy drew in a deep breath and stretched in her chair. By now Stan Jones and his two men were safely behind bars. Once she and the Hardys had disarmed them, George had untied Soong and Jeff and then run to a phone and contacted both the police and Tim An. Not ten minutes after that, Jones and his men were in custody, and Nancy, George, Frank, Joe, Jeff, and Soong were on their way to the police station to give their statements. Since they'd gotten back to the consulate, they had been filling in Tim An and April on what Stan had been up to, and why.

"I can't believe he and Rupert Tran thought they could use these sorts of scare tactics to force me to resign," the president said, shaking his head sadly.

"Stan is hotheaded," April said. "And Rupert is willing to take the advice of his friend, even though he shouldn't."

"I can't believe I was stupid enough not to see what was going on," Jeff put in. "Then again, I didn't know Stan in Philonesia. I just made a mistake in believing him when he said he wanted to be my friend."

"Dean Harper was happy to know that Jones is behind bars, that's for sure," Frank Hardy said.

"The whole time, he wanted to use Ethics Now as a cover for committing attacks on the medical labs in the hopes they would scare Jeff into returning home," Joe explained. "He even set the fire that we found Jeff putting out the day of the earthquake. With Stan in jail, and the other members committed to more pacifist tactics, the university shouldn't have any more trouble with Ethics Now."

Frank thought of a last question. "Stan says he wasn't the one who tipped off the police to us, though. So who did?"

A small voice piped up. "That was me," Charlene Hilton said. When they'd returned to the consulate, Nancy was a bit surprised to see that Charlene, Li, and Erik were still there, but apparently they couldn't bring themselves to leave without knowing what had happened to Soong.

"Remember when someone spray-painted Dean Harper?" she asked the Hardys. When Frank nodded, Charlene went on. "That was me."

"You were the spray-painting attacker?" Joe asked.

"Remember, you said it was a woman," Frank put in.

"Right." Joe urged Charlene to go on.

Charlene tossed back her blond hair. "Well, after I attacked the dean, I got a good look at both you guys. I recognized you the second you came to our meeting, but I decided not to say anything to the group until I knew what was up. I guess I figured that if you were Nancy's friends, you were probably okay. And I could tell you didn't want to commit the action, so when Stan gave me the details of your action, I called the police and tipped them off. That way, you wouldn't have to go through with it, I figured." Charlene blushed. "Of course, I also didn't know what a creep Stan was." She swallowed hard. "I think he must have been the one who stole Soong's schedule. The whole time he was using me. Boy, oh boy, if anyone was stupid, it was me. I hope I never ever see that weirdo again. And if I do, he'd better watch out."

"Don't feel bad," said Frank. "Stan had a lot of us going. What matters most is that the mysteries are solved and Soong An is safe."

Nancy saw him giving Soong a long look, as she nestled in Jeffrey's arms. It couldn't be easy for Frank Hardy to accept that Soong An really was in love with Jeff, after everything that had happened. She gave him a reassuring hug and said to the group, "Frank's right. Soong is safe. That's what is most important."

"And that she was able to win the competition, fair and square." Erik reached over to give his friend a kiss on the cheek. "Miles isn't happy, but that's okay."

"Why?" Soong said.

Erik smiled. "Because I fired him."

"You didn't!" Soong An's eyes were wide with amusement.

"I did," Erik confirmed. "And he deserved it."

"You can always get another manager," Soong said.

"That's right," Erik agreed. "Maybe I'll even do better in my career. I'll come back next year—and win."

Soong laughed. Jeffrey kissed her lingeringly, and then the couple smiled tenderly at each other. Tim An coughed uncomfortably. "I suppose I must get used to all this," he said. "Clearly Soong An's will is stronger than my own."

"That's right," Soong said, grinning mischievously. "You had better get used to it."

"Why is that?" April asked.

"Because I have a promising career ahead of me in this country," Soong said, "and I plan to make the most of it."

THE HARDY BOYS CASEFILES

☐ #1: DEAD ON TARGET	73992-1/$3.99	☐ #64: ENDANGERED SPECIES	73100-9/$3.99
☐ #2: EVIL, INC.	73668-X/$3.99	☐ #65: NO MERCY	73101-7/$3.99
☐ #3: CULT OF CRIME	68726-3/$3.75	☐ #66: THE PHOENIX EQUATION	73102-5/$3.99
☐ #4: THE LAZARUS PLOT	73995-6/$3.75	☐ #68: ROUGH RIDING	73104-1/$3.75
☐ #5: EDGE OF DESTRUCTION	73669-8/$3.99	☐ #69: MAYHEM IN MOTION	73105-X/$3.75
☐ #6: THE CROWNING OF TERROR	73670-1/$3.50	☐ #71: REAL HORROR	73107-6/$3.99
		☐ #72: SCREAMERS	73108-4/$3.75
☐ #7: DEATHGAME	73672-8/$3.99	☐ #73: BAD RAP	73109-2/$3.99
☐ #8: SEE NO EVIL	73673-6/$3.50	☐ #74: ROAD PIRATES	73110-6/$3.99
☐ #9: THE GENIUS THIEVES	73674-4/$3.50	☐ #75: NO WAY OUT	73111-4/$3.99
☐ #12: PERFECT GETAWAY	73675-2/$3.50	☐ #76: TAGGED FOR TERROR	73112-2/$3.99
☐ #13: THE BORGIA DAGGER	73676-0/$3.50	☐ #77: SURVIVAL RUN	79461-2/$3.99
☐ #14: TOO MANY TRAITORS	73677-9/$3.50	☐ #78: THE PACIFIC CONSPIRACY	79462-0/$3.99
☐ #16: THICK AS THIEVES	74663-4/$3.50	☐ #79: DANGER UNLIMITED	79463-9/$3.99
☐ #30: THE DEADLIEST DARE	74613-8/$3.50	☐ #80: DEAD OF NIGHT	79464-7/$3.99
☐ #32: BLOOD MONEY	74665-0/$3.50	☐ #81: SHEER TERROR	79465-5/$3.99
☐ #33: COLLISION COURSE	74666-9/$3.50	☐ #82: POISONED PARADISE	79466-3/$3.99
☐ #35: THE DEAD SEASON	74105-5/$3.50	☐ #83: TOXIC REVENGE	79467-1/$3.99
☐ #37: DANGER ZONE	73751-1/$3.75	☐ #84: FALSE ALARM	79468-X/$3.99
☐ #41: HIGHWAY ROBBERY	70038-3/$3.75	☐ #85: WINNER TAKE ALL	79469-8/$3.99
☐ #42: THE LAST LAUGH	74614-6/$3.50	☐ #86: VIRTUAL VILLAINY	79470-1/$3.99
☐ #44: CASTLE FEAR	74615-4/$3.75	☐ #87: DEAD MAN IN DEADWOOD	79471-X/$3.99
☐ #45: IN SELF-DEFENSE	70042-1/$3.75	☐ #88: INFERNO OF FEAR	79472-8/$3.99
☐ #47: FLIGHT INTO DANGER	70044-8/$3.99	☐ #89: DARKNESS FALLS	79473-6/$3.99
☐ #48: ROCK 'N' REVENGE	70045-6/$3.50	☐ #90: DEADLY ENGAGEMENT	79474-4/$3.99
☐ #49: DIRTY DEEDS	70046-4/$3.99	☐ #91: HOT WHEELS	79475-2/$3.99
☐ #50: POWER PLAY	70047-2/$3.99	☐ #92: SABOTAGE AT SEA	79476-0/$3.99
☐ #52: UNCIVIL WAR	70049-9/$3.50	☐ #93: MISSION: MAYHEM	88204-X/$3.99
☐ #53: WEB OF HORROR	73089-4/$3.99	☐ #94: A TASTE FOR TERROR	88205-8/$3.99
☐ #54: DEEP TROUBLE	73090-8/$3.99	☐ #95: ILLEGAL PROCEDURE	88206-6/$3.99
☐ #55: BEYOND THE LAW	73091-6/$3.50	☐ #96: AGAINST ALL ODDS	88207-4/$3.99
☐ #56: HEIGHT OF DANGER	73092-4/$3.50	☐ #97: PURE EVIL	88208-2/$3.99
☐ #57: TERROR ON TRACK	73093-2/$3.99	☐ #98: MURDER BY MAGIC	88209-0/$3.99
☐ #60: DEADFALL	73096-7/$3.75	☐ #99: FRAME-UP	88210-4/$3.99
☐ #61: GRAVE DANGER	73097-5/$3.99	☐ #100: TRUE THRILLER	88211-2/$3.99
☐ #62: FINAL GAMBIT	73098-3/$3.75	☐ #101: PEAK OF DANGER	88212-0/$3.99
☐ #63: COLD SWEAT	73099-1/$3.75	☐ #102: WRONG SIDE OF THE LAW	88213-9/$3.99

Simon & Schuster Mail Order
200 Old Tappan Rd., Old Tappan, N.J. 07675

Please send me the books I have checked above. I am enclosing $_____ (please add $0.75 to cover the postage and handling for each order. Please add appropriate sales tax). Send check or money order–no cash or C.O.D.'s please. Allow up to six weeks for delivery. For purchase over $10.00 you may use VISA: card number, expiration date and customer signature must be included.

Name _____

Address _____

City _____ State/Zip _____

VISA Card # _____ Exp.Date _____

Signature _____ 762-25